I0645257

At Daytrap

(Tales from a Farmhouse near Daytrap)

In Case Of Emergency Press

http://www.icoe.com.au

At Daytrap

(Tales from a Farmhouse near Daytrap)
Believed to be written by
Reginald Wells
With an Afterword and Memoir by
Sir Pelham Corrie

Published by In Case of Emergency Press 2013

ISBN 978-0-9943525-5-2

Malcontents

"Despite everything he was a loving man, a man with much to give mankind and womankind, a man who in fact did give, who gave until it hurt. And yet, the world was ungrateful, and even contemptuous. Inevitably he was hurt, and hurt again, and again, and again, and again."

(from the papers of Reginald Wells)

THE PIG

a true story

An Uncle Vern story: Parental Guidance Recommended

My parents were in a hurry as usual and when they dropped me at the gate of Uncle Vern and Auntie Mona's farm they did not wait but simply asked me to say hello for them. "We'll be back in two weeks!" my mother said from the moving car as I closed the door. I waved until they rounded the bend. I don't think they looked back but I couldn't be sure because the road was very dusty. There being no one to greet, me I climbed over the gate and headed for the farmhouse.

Since my last holidays Uncle Vern had enjoyed a small measure of fame, or notoriety, on account of a controversial business venture. A man of boundless energy, always trying to think of ways of bettering mankind's lot, he had heard that, as well as dogs for the blind, you could get dogs for the deaf who would answer the phone for you and converse with visitors in your lieu if you were hard of hearing.

Uncle Vern's idea was to have dogs for the dumb as well. He figured that many people who were dumb, especially the violently dumb, would be better citizens if they had dogs to help them, dogs that were dumber and more violent than they were. He had chosen bull terriers and appeared to have a thriving business until the authorities stepped in.

I knew about these things because he had sent the newspaper clippings to me at school. In his letter he had said, "Just think, Reg, how different life would be for many ordinary, downtrodden Australians if they were able to feel important, if they could have just a bit of friendship and companionship from their dog, and some long-needed respect from John Q. Public. They can get all this and more just by walking down the street with their beautiful, fully-trained pit bull. Every man could walk abroad and feel like a Captain of Industry knowing that he had something very dumb and very powerful under his control!" The newspaper saw things differently, of course, and sided very obviously with the RSPCA and the Health Department in the affair.

These matters must have taken up much of Uncle Vern's time of late because what I saw as I walked up the long drive was far from cheering. The sheep had not been shorn in fifteen months and were in serious need of dagging, at the least. Some stood round in small listless groups and others paced rapidly back and forth. In a nearby, thistle-infested paddock a large number of young bulls, destined to become steers, snorted and jostled each other. In the main paddock Desmond the big bull was busy with the cows. Even from a distance one could see that they had lost condition and that pink-eye was rife. Way, way off at the top end of the bottom paddock I saw a small figure - Uncle Vern, undoubtedly - working on the riverbank with his tractor, combating either silting or erosion, it was hard to tell which.

As I neared the farmhouse the air was redolent of molten fat. Auntie Mona was making soap. Things had been tough in the rural sector for some time, but I knew I wouldn't hear any complaints from Auntie Mona or Uncle Vern. They were not the sort of people to whinge about drought as soon as the water stopped dripping from their hats. No matter what happened, life went on, and on.

I found Auntie Mona in the laundry, not unexpectedly, stirring the copper.

"Reggie!" she said. "We thought you might be coming. I can't kiss you, Reg, I'm covered in fat. But come to the kitchen and have a cup of tea!"

Over a cuppa Auntie Mona explained that Uncle Vern was putting a corduroy on the riverbanks, but that he ought to be back soon, and that she wasn't sure what he would like to do in the afternoon.

I knew what he would like to do, though.

Uncle Vern liked nothing better than to go out to his toolshed, pull his old stool up to the shucking bucket and commence to tell a yarn. Naturally he liked to have someone to tell it to: there was nothing I liked better than to avoid him at these times. But it was not always possible.

Presently the tractor approached. I tried to slip away but the flyscreen on the kitchen door squeaked and Auntie Mona noticed the time and said to me,

"Reginald, go and give your Uncle a hand with the chooks."

I knew what she meant: keep an eye on him. I didn't like it, but I was a good lad, so I went. She was, after all, my mother's sister.

By the time I got there the chooks were gathering excitedly at the toolshed door, drawn by the sound of the maize hitting the tin . Normally they scattered before me but here I had to kick them out of the way to get in. Uncle Vern was singing fitfully.

"Mother and daughter too,

Working for the yankee dolllaaaar!

(It's da troot, man, da troot!)"

"Ah Reginald, you have come for another instalment of the family chronicles. File this," he said, handing me his maize and rasp as he pulled out the makings.

          An Uncle Vern story: Parental Guidance Recommended

The chooks by this stage were in a frenzy of expectation, though Uncle Vern seemed oblivious of them.

"Treat 'em mean, Keep 'em keen" , that was his motto. As he took his first drag on the shag he said,

"I have been remiss in that I have never told you about your great-great-grandfather Rodney. Now there was a man's man. A real bushman, my word he was. He spent most of his life in the bush. Cutting sleepers, dogging, seed collecting, milking, he did it all. He even worked for a year, in the butter factory at Yarragon.

"But what he loved best was humping his bluey with his mates in the bush. He knocked about with old Cyril Mustard and Roy Grogan. They thought nothing of heading bush for three or six months to try their luck at this show or that, to get out there back o' beyond and rough it together. Men in a man's country!

"Now I know what you're thinking but it wasn't like that, that wasn't invented in them days, not in this country at least, and they knew nothing of it. Frankly, son, it was a good thing too, or nothing might have ever got done. All this," he said waving grandly towards the paddocks of thin pasture, "all this might still be unproductive, virgin bush! In a way, Reg, it was ignorance that made this country what it is today, and that is worth remembering. A little learning is a dangerous thing!

"Anyhow, one year they were up Big Flat Creek Track working a small molybdenum mine. On this occasion they took a piglet with them. It was old Cyril's idea and they all agreed it was a good one. They used to get sick of kangaroo and wallaby, and they thought they'd have a nice bit of pork as well. But it didn't work out that way as you shall see.

"The pig followed them everywhere. It was just like a dog! It wagged its tail. It had personality. It had a sense of humour. It laughed at their jokes. It joined in their games and learnt to smoke a pipe just like them and it slept with them at night.

"As time went by they could not help becoming fond of their pig. Against their original determination they gave the pig a name. It was a girl pig so they called her Teresa, after the saint. They might have been rough men, but they never forgot their religion.

"Well, like I was saying, as she got older, Teresa got bigger, and as she got bigger great-great grandad Rodney and the other men began to notice things about her. She was, by then, about the same size as a human person. They saw that she was pink and hairy, like a woman, and curvaceous, like a woman. She could be coy and play hard-to-get, as a woman can and she had other attributes that a woman has.

"One night they had a little party. They had grown some watermelons down by the river and in some of these watermelons they had made a brew. Teresa, being unused to drinking, passed out before the men. One minute she was laughing, the next she was lying on her side snoring softly and smiling beatifically. From time to time she grunted as she dreamed and her little tail flicked this way and that in a most provocative manner. The men grew very pensive, very pensive indeed.

"In the pale, deceptive moonlight her pink gams shone invitingly. The three men had been friends a long time, through thick and thin, and they were not about to fall out over a thing like this. They were, after all, civilized men, not beasts. So what they did was they agreed that the following night would be Cyril's turn, and the night after that, great-great-grandad Rodney's; and after that young Roy's and so on and that night they would all have a go.

"Now, you must remember, times have changed considerable since those days. That was the bush. Nowadays, sure, it's all press-a-button-bend-over-and-away-ya-go. Those were gumnut and damper days. You did what you could because that was all you could do.. There were no newspapers or magazines or psychotherapists to tell them that it was wrong to divide the pig up in this way....nevertheless, like many of the old-fashioned things, it worked, and they lived happily with Teresa for some time.

"As they say," said Uncle Vern, "everything which goes up comes together, and after a while your great-great- grandfather Rodney began to have his doubts. He was a Catholic man and he realized that Teresa did not have an immortal soul.

"One night, when Teresa was asleep, he broached the matter with his mates around the old campfire.

"'Fond as I am of Teresa - and you know how fond I am of her -' he said, 'you must admit that she has her limitations as a woman.'

"'Like what!?' challenged the ever-loyal Roy.

"Rodney did not wish to go into things metaphysical like the soul which would have gone soaring over Roy's head.

"'Well, for one thing,' he said, 'she can't cook.'

"They pushed and prodded at the fire with their bush pokers as they pondered this. Then Rodney made a further announcement

"'Tomorrow I am going to Eden and I will be back within the week with a proper cook!'

"'Does this mean we get to have your nights with Teresa?' asked Roy excitedly.

          An Uncle Vern story: Parental Guidance Recommended

"'Not so loud!' hissed Cyril,'You'll wake her!'

"'Roy,' said Rodney patiently, 'we are Socialists, and as we have always shared everything, so we shall share the new cook.'

"'It's going to be an awkward draw,' said Cyril.

"'No, Cyril, I'm saying that after I get back we will, I mean Teresa will no longer...'

"'Good God, man, we can't eat her!' exclaimed Cyril.

"'What d'you take me for, Cyril?! Of course not! Alls what I mean is that from then on Teresa will just be our friend.'

"This announcement was something of a shock to young Roy. Cyril comforted him as best he could. Roy was soon asleep in his swag.

"Cyril lay in his swag, still awake. Rodney sat up poking at the coals.

"'Rodney,' said Cyril.

"'Yes, Cyril,' said Rodney.

"'You will make sure she's not the full twobob, won't you?'

"'Cyril, I know what I'm doing,' said Rodney.

"'Sorry, Rodney,' said Cyril, 'Goodnight!'

"'Goodnight, Cyril,' said Rodney.

"Rodney waited a while and then, for the last time, he approached Teresa the way a man in his prime approaches a very attractive pig.

"Ten days later Rodney returned from Eden with the new cook. The other men were neither surprised nor disappointed that the new cook, whose name was Connie, bore a striking resemblance to Teresa. The new camp arrangements were soon settled. Connie was no great chef, but she was quite adequate as a cook. Teresa, to the men's surprise, adapted remarkably quickly to the new regime and beyond the third day did not need to be tied down at all. The men were relieved and gratified that Connie and Teresa seemed to get along well.

"About two weeks later Connie was in the swag with grandad Rodney when she woke him urgently and demanded,

"'What was that noise?'

"Rodney knew at once what it was: it was Teresa in the throes of passion. He placated Connie.

"'Teresa is a noisy sleeper,' he said, 'she is dreaming.'

"The next morning, down at the mine, Rodney confronted his two mates.

"'What's been going on, then?'

                 An Uncle Vern story: Parental Guidance Recommended

"Under the pressure of his questioning they broke down and confessed that they had both continued to see Teresa. Great-great-grandfather Rodney looked them both squarely in the eye and spoke softly. He was dangerous when he spoke softly.

"'How long has this been going on?'

"'Since last Tuesday,' said a chastened Cyril.

"'You know what this means?' Rodney said to Roy.

"'What?' asked Roy.

"'I am owed three nights!'

"As Cyril had predicted, the draw had become awkward. But they were mates: they worked it out equitably and for the next couple of months the camp ran smoothly enough.

"Then, one ill-starred night, Connie heard Roy's reedy voicy cry out.

"'Oh! Teresa, Teresa, oh! Oh! OH! Teresa I love you!!'

"She sat up and saw at the far side of the camp Roy and Teresa in an intimate embrace. Enraged, she flew at him with a burning brand she snatched from the fire.

"'You two-timing bastard!' she said as she hit him where it would do the most damage, giving him scars that he took to his grave. By then Roger and Cyril, realizing what had happened, had thrown her to the ground. She was extremely hysterical and hard to hold, and, as they observed, she was far from unattractive when roused. Roger and Cyril were forced to spend the best part of the night comforting the poor woman, while young Roy - lucky devil - comforted Teresa.

"In the hard morning they woke late. There would be no work at the mine that morning. Connie was still angry. She fully realized what had been going on right under her very nose and she delivered her ultimatum:

"' Either that pig goes or I go!'

"The men instantly understood that this was a matter that would require considerable thought and discussion. They stood around looking at each other.

"'Whaddaya reckon?" asked Roy'

"Cyril looked at Rodney. Teresa stood some distance away, discreetly peeking out from the bracken, her snout moist, her little tail wagging hopefully. Rodney waited a decent interval before speaking.

"'If ya follow that creek two miles upstream,' he said to Connie, in the friendliest possible way, 'ya know, the way we came in...'

"Silent and furious, Connie gathered her things. Then, in a last ditch effort, she said to the men desperately,

"' But I'm expecting! What about the baby?'

"Great-great-grandfather Rodney, a shrewd man, looked at her for a few moments to see if she were lying, and then he said,

"'That's ok, you can keep it.'

"He knew he had made the right decision."

By this time the chooks were absolutely beside themselves and making a huge racket. Uncle Vern stood up and hitched his trousers.

"Haven't you finished yet?" he inquired in the derisive tone that with him meant friendliness.

My bucket was full. I always managed to fill a bucket when listening to Uncle Vern's yarns. Who wouldn't?

As we went into the farmhouse he said in his low voice of confidence, "I've got a coupla new videos ya might enjoy watchin' after Auntie Mona goes to bed."

Already I knew that these holidays would be no different than all the rest.

ROY AND THE HAG

an unbelievable story

An Uncle Vern Story. Strictly Adults Only.

Fishing was another of Uncle Vern's passions. No holiday would be complete without at least one perfectly good day being wasted on a dreary and pointless fishing expedition which invariably ended in disaster.

I innocently wandered into the kitchen still rubbing the sleep from my eyes and spotted Uncle Vern's dirty, old, weed-entangled rod lying on the table. Then, at once, without I even approach the trencher of bacon and eggs with Worcestershire sauce on a bed of porridge ("Always ship a good load o' ballast before tackling the briney," Uncle Vern always said,) before I even smelled the formidable repast that Auntie Mona always prepared on fishing expedition mornings, the attack of biliousness struck.

Half an hour later Auntie Mona was at the toilet door. "Reginald," she coaxed, "Reggie, Uncle Vern only wants to bond with you. You know how much it means to him. Please Reggie, it's only one day..."

Only one day!

     An Uncle Vern Story. Strictly Adults Only.

"But Auntie Mona," I protested forlornly, "it says in the Bible that a day in hell is longer than an eternity on earth..." It wasn't true but I had to say something. Then she began to blubber about not being able to have any children.

Before long my Uncle and I were in his leaky, old tinny, Vern opening his first alcohol supplement for the day and me pulling as best I could on the oars which he had waggishly carved into phalluses. The bait was higher that the cirrus clouds creeping across the sky above us and I kept it close by me as I knew from bitter experience that my Uncle would soon remove his boots.

He pulled some stray shag from his cracked lips and commenced another of his inevitable yarns.

"You know, Reggie, it was on a day not unlike this that Young Roy, cousin Roy, poor tragic Roy, did not go into the Wallabong pub. It was a beautiful, sunny, still, early autumn day, unseasonally warm for that time of year. The dark, womblike interior of the hotel bar beckoned. Through the walls he heard faintly the inviting laughter of the men within, and from the airconditioner came the intimate and friendly aroma of stale smoke and slops, calling him with their age-old power, to come on in and keep them company as he did every day when he was not incapable of raising himself from his sick bed.

"As he stood outside the pub Roy accidentally saw his reflection in the windows. He looked old and sick. He felt old and sick. 'Who cares', he thought, darkly.

"Roy walked past the bar and into the bottleshop. He bought himself half-a-dozen beers and a bottle of port. Then he wandered down to the jetty, the long way, avoiding the hotel.

"It was the off season. The jetty was deserted. A line of rowboats rocked on the water by the launching ramp. The sun shone from a cloudless cerulean sky onto still, aquamarine water and hazy, azure hills. How'd ya like them words boy?"

"Real good, Uncle Vern," I said, like I always did. "But what do they mean?"

"Don't interrupt the flow, Reg! Casually, Roy looked through all the boats until he found one with oars and oarlocks. It was a poor looking lapstreak, so he took the oars and oarlocks out of it and put them on a decent looking boat and took off with his sustenance.

"At first he rowed swiftly with long, powerful strokes. But it had been some time since he had been fit so he stopped a hundred yards from shore and took off his jumper. He rolled up his sleeves and had a little rest. Then he began rowing again, more slowly, heading for the entrance to the lakes, heading for the open sea.

                    An Uncle Vern Story. Strictly Adults Only.

"The water was as still as a glass eye in an ice block. A mile or so away he could see the lighthouse. It had been some time since he had been out there and he decided to row to it. There and back would be a good day's work.

"Clearing the bar he shipped oars and let the current carry him towards the island. Always let the water do it for ya. He knew it would. Roy was a seaman's seaman. He rolled a smoke and opened a beer.

"He lay back in the boat and closed his eyes and soaked up the warmth of the sun. The water lapped hypnotically against the hull. Occasionally he heard the plaintive cry of a plover or a gull and it reminded him of the torments that heaved and rumbled dimly beneath the surface of his apparently untroubled brow, torments which he never allowed to bother him under any circumstances and he drifted off into slumber. The morning's exertions had left him completely fagged.

"When he woke to the sound of the breaking sea he found he had drifted to the north of the island and was quickly being blown towards it by the wind which had swung around shoreward. Desperately he rowed away from certain disaster. After a few minutes of superhuman effort he was more or less safe."

Uncle Vern stopped talking. A vacant look came into his eyes, an intense look of concentration. His upper body leant to one side so that its weight was now resting on one buttock. He was about to forget himself. I took a deep breath. There was a deafening report and a rush of hot, stinking air engulfed the boat. Through the heat haze I saw Uncle Vern recover his senses and smile. Tears came to my eyes and my lungs screamed for air.

"How'd ya like that one, Reggie," leered Uncle Vern. I dared not speak and could but nod to him and smile, somewhat grimly, I fear. "It's workin' real good since I had it rebored!" said Uncle Vern rather airily.

"Where was I?" asked Uncle Vern. "Oh, yes, Roy had escaped from the pounding breakers. Breathing heavily he rested, exhausted, on his oars, conscious only of the blood throbbing madly in his temples. He had not even the strength to open a stubby."

I could hold my breath no longer and gasped for air, breaking my stroke and interrupting Uncle Vern's narrative.

"Good heavens Reginald, what are you doing? I wish you'd keep your mind on the job."

"Sorry Uncle Vern," I said.

"That's all right. Don't worry about it. Bodily motions can't be helped," (He always said that.) Uncle Vern continued,

"Gradually Roy regained his senses and found that he was staring at a solitary rock sticking up out of the water. Dipping an oar he turned the craft and rowed towards it.

"The waters there seemed calmer. There might be mussels and oysters there with which to build his strength. It was only mid-afternoon and there was plenty of time.

"Distances over water are extremely deceptive. The rock proved far larger, and far further away than he had expected. But he pressed on, rested halfway, restored his natural vigour with a beer and kept rowing.

"As he approached the rock he saw something very queer.

"What had at first looked like a bird, a large black bird, like a cormorant, or a shag, was in fact an old woman. And extremely old woman. She was dressed in rags and apparently asleep. In the bearing of the pathetic rag and weed bedraggled figure there was a suggestion of all the misery that ever happened in the world and of a profound resignation such as is found only in those who watch television or read newspapers.

"Ideas were forming in Roy's mind. Quietly he dropped his anchor. Very, very carefully - for he knew from personal experience how the sound of a port bottle cork popping could rouse even those who had for many hours seemed dead and half decomposed - very, very carefully he opened the port and took a swig and wiped his mouth delicately with the back of his hand.

"In the bar there had been stories told among the seafarers of a vanishing rock, a malevolent presence somewhere in the vicinity of the lighthouse. But he had never given anything anyone in the bar said any real credence. Not that he had ever thought about the things they said in a critical way, he was not a hypocritical sort of person.

"He took another swig and silently rolled a smoke. He smoked it and watched the old woman.

"The sun was going down. Her silhouette reminded him of a mermaid he had seen in a picture of Copenhagen in one of them foreign art magazines. The shore was not far away and he was not worried about the time. He was fascinated instead by the green gold gleam the light of the setting sun lent the woman's face and arms. Her wrinkles had vanished

    An Uncle Vern Story. Strictly Adults Only.

and he noticed with some quickening of interest that she had good bone structure.

"Roy mused. A woman, he thought, only needed one good feature, really. A man had to be brave, strong, tough, decisive, carefree, hunky, a good drinker, and omniscient, but a woman only needed one good quality. He always tried to look for this quality in a woman. It might be a smile, or an expression, an accent, a limp, hair, a minor lisp or a squint, money or a house...he took another swig...she was looking better all the time.

"Then she opened her eyes. The woman's eyes had, yes, a radiance that stabbed him through his heart, that transfixed him like a butterfly stuck in the box with a pin. And she wore lipstick, he now saw. It was as if scales had fallen from his eyes. The whole world became luminous. Colours were enhanced. The spray from the water on the rocks danced like electric diamonds and burnt his skin where it touched him just like sheepdip on an open sore. He felt the surge of the tide, the urge of the moon, the quickness of shoals of fish and the proud, reassuring, thrusting presence of the lighthouse.

"The woman was not sixty, and if she was fifty you'd hardly have believed it. Her rags were not seaweed but leather, expensive, fancy-tooled Italian leather. Roy liked the wet look. Through the many shredded patches of her garment he saw her firm, generous limbs, washed with seawater and suntan lotion, well sprung, primed for action...

"Not a word was spoken. Words, Roy realized, were unnecessary. That was the way he liked it. Quickly he weighed anchor and rowed to the rock, securing his boat again with a tremulous hand

"She was a few feet away, not 35 years old and despite the bizarre clothes, on close inspection she was a doll, a total doll.

"Hello," she said.

"For what happened next Roy was not entirely responsible. It would not be an exaggeration to say that for a time he became completely bereft of his senses. Every living cell of his body was awakened. Things happened in the rowboat that he could barely describe later. How long it all took we'll never know but as the Bible says, 'a day in paradise is worth an eternity on earth.'

"At the moment of what was for Roy the climax of the experience he hugged her to him and closed his eyes and smiled joyfully, his manhood satisfied and, to be blunt, quite spent.

"And when he opened his eyes again he found that he was hugging an old hag covered in weeds. He was horrified and tried to fling her from him but she clung

                    An Uncle Vern Story. Strictly Adults Only.

tight, apparently asleep. With all his manly might Roy freed himself of her grip and flung her onto the rock.

"' But Rodney..' she said

"Roy had been cunning enough not to give his right name. But the sea was rising and the sky was lowering and the sun was almost gone.

"'Rodney!' she cried, 'I am the only daughter of a rich Italian fruiterer. If you but take me to shore I will marry you and we will live happily ever after!' or words to that effect.

"Roy rowed. He swigged some port and rowed. She kept singing out to him like a siren. Her assets were considerable, it seemed, and she was beginning to look attractive again. But the sea was now fierce. Roy was no fool. There was something fishy about her story, and he was not going to buy a pig in a poke. He called to her, 'Why don't you bloody well swim to shore?'

"' I can't swim!' she cried.

"He heard her words but faintly above the raging sea. Roy remembered that he could not swim either.

"Cousin Roy swung the boat back around towards the rock but in the dark a freak wave picked up Roy and his boat and dropped them into the sea. The sea rose and covered the rock. The last thing Roy did, with his last ounce of consciousness, was cling to the upturned hull with a grip fierce as rigor mortis."

Uncle Vern held up his stubby to demonstrate ferocity of grip, and as he did so he toppled out of the boat almost capsizing it. "Help!" he screamed, "Help! I can't swim!" The river was only two and a half feet deep, but there was no point in telling Vern this as he was in a state of panic. Wildly he grasped the gunwales like a madman, putting all his weight on the starboard side as he tried to throw one of his polio-withered legs aboard and in a moment of confusion all was lost, and we were both in the river and the tinny had taken so much water it sank.

Uncle Vern is a fairly tall man and the water barely reached his chest yet there he was thrashing his arms and legs around and screaming, "Mona help! Help, Mona I'm drowning! Mona! Mona!" I ducked down into the water and pulled out one of his beers. As I snapped off the top Uncle Vern suddenly regained his composure, accepted the beer, poured some down his throat and continued his story.

"The beams of the lighthouse swung blindly back and forth above them like lost hope."

He belched.

"Late in the afternoon of the next day a search party looking for the missing rowboat found Roy's prostrate

                        An Uncle Vern Story. Strictly Adults Only.

body on the beach beside the upturned boat. He was still clinging to the port bottle, a testament to the tenacity of the will to drink.

"As he recovered they told him about the miraculous rescue of the Italian fruit heiress who had spent the night clinging to a rock just below the hightide line.

"Roy tried to tell them about her, as much as he could tell without giving too much away but they all laughed at him and thought he was just telling another one of his stories."

"Old hag?" they said. "You've got the wrong one Roy, Luisa's a doll!"

Uncle Vern looked down at the sunken boat.

"Stuff it," he said phlegmatically as he set off down the river. "We might as well walk home. Just keep your eye peeled for stingrays. Gee, I'm sorry, Reginald. Today I was gonna show ya my special eel hole. Hardly anyone knows where it is and all ya have to do is reach in and pull out as many big, fat eels as ya want. Auntie Mona loves it when I bring her home a big, fat eel."

I was soaked to the skin. It was quite lucky, really. A couple of sneezes when I got home and I could tell Auntie Mona I had pneumonia and be confined to bed for maybe three or four days. As we trudged back up the river I found myself wondering, as I had so often in the past, why Uncle Vern told me these stories.

   An Uncle Vern Story. Strictly Adults Only.

THE ASIAN BRIDE

a tirade

An Uncle Vern Story: Unfit for Human Consumption

Early one morning Flaps the dog and I went down to the highway to check the fridge that served as a mailbox for Uncle Vern and Auntie Mona. As we dawdled down the long, dusty drive, between the ranks of lemon-scented gums, a host of bellbirds piped and chimed, proclaiming the sundrenched day. Though the air was walled with their song, try as I might I could never catch a glimpse of even one of these elusive birds.

There was no letter from my parents, alas, just the latest "Hoofs 'n' Horns" for Uncle Vern. As we approached the farmhouse we heard an argument in progress. I did not eavesdrop but I could not help hearing a few inconsequential phrases from Auntie Mona.

"...told me you...filthy thing near...swear that's the..."

A long, pink thing flew out the kitchen window and into the rosemary bush.

The flywire door slammed shut and Uncle Vern limped angrily to the rosemary bush, retrieved the pink thing and then repaired to his toolshed. Flaps and I laid low for a few minutes and entered the kitchen cautiously.

"Hi Auntie Mona, here's..."

"Put it down and get out, Reginald!" she said harshly. "I have had enough of men today, quite enough and that even includes you! Go and find your Uncle in the toolshed if you want something to do!"

"What's he doing down there, Auntie Mona?" I asked.

"What he always bloody does Reginald, he's tending the great unknown!"

I had never heard Auntie Mona use strong language before and it was somewhat shocking. Flaps and I walked slowly down to the toolshed as we did not want to arrive at an inopportune moment. When we got there Flaps had a quick look inside and ran away. Perhaps I should have done the same. I stood in the doorway waiting for Uncle Vern to notice I was there.

But he was so engrossed in his activity that he didn't see me. I watched as he had a large sip of his stubby and then replaced it with practised ease in the refrigerator he had wisely installed out there when he had first married Auntie Mona. He went to the gas bottle and tightened the connection to the portable gas stove. He went back to the fridge and had another sip then put the large copper pot on the stove. Next he took the bucket to the fridge and had another drink and then poured the water into the copper. Then he went back to the fridge and opened another stubby and had a mouthful and put it back and got a box of matches out of his pocket and went back to the fridge and had another sip of beer. He went then to the stove and turned on the gas and then got some more refreshment from the refrigerator, and then went to the stove and lit it. There was a huge explosion as a flame of gas spread through the toolshed. An overpowering smell of singed hair oppressed the room. I am not sure when he noticed I was there but after draining his stubby he began to declaim, loudly and aggressively, as if he wanted Auntie Mona in the kitchen to hear,

"THE WHITE WOMAN HAS PRICED HERSELF RIGHT OUT OF THE MARRIAGE MARKET!"

He was in a bad mood. He wrenched another beer from the fridge.

"What is wrong with the white woman?" he demanded fiercely of the bench drill. He turned to me and asked rhetorically, "Who does she think she is? What does she think she is playing at, eh? Eh? I don't mind telling you Reggie I am in a bad mood and I am gonna catch something, I'm gonna kill it and pluck it and eat it. I'm gonna stuff it and cook it and eat it! By God I'll cut it and cook it and salt it and eat it!

"The white woman, mark my words Reg, even though I know a farmer is without honour in his own loungeroom, mark my words, the white woman will have to wake up to herself or make way for them that knows what end of the sausage is up!

"Look at Joe Blake's wife! Ups and walks out on her God-given husband of thirty-seven years at age fifty-two and why? Why? I'll tell you why Reg: for no bloody reason, that's why! It's women like that give women a bad name, Reg, and that hurts me. It hurts me. I want women to be nice Reg...and I want to be nice to them. I want them to have everything. I want to give them things Reg, do you understand what I am trying to say? I want them to be nice and respectable because I respect women and I care for them and I protect them.

"Have you ever heard me use bad language in front of the weaker sex, Reg? No, you haven't, and you never will because I never do. It's the way I was brought up. My father on his deathbed made me promise him two things. 'Vern,' he said, 'I am going to a better place - the grave - but you must stay here in Daytrap, and I want you to do two things for me. Never use bad language in front of the weaker sex, and never give your right name to them that don't know better.' I have honoured his dying wishes, Reg and I never swear in front of women and I hate - hate! - a man who does so without justification..."

Uncle Vern's eye's bulged like golfballs. His thyroid condition was in danger of getting out of hand. Fortunately I knew what to do.

"Manilla, Uncle Vern," I said.

The effect was instantaneous. An air of calm came over him.

"Manilla? Ah, yes indeed, you're getting on to a wavelength, Reggie. You're coming along boy. Manilla! Aaaah, Manilla!"

A faraway look came into his eyes.

"You see things in Manilla, Reg, that would make every part of your Christian body stand on end. There is a street in Manilla, Reg, where you can get anything you can imagine and hundreds and hundreds of other things as well, just for money. You could easily spend everything you've got just window shopping. In one week I used forty-two bottles of my heart pills and I never felt better in all my life. Gender mobility. You ever heard of that, Reg?"

"No, Uncle Vern," I said.

"Well, never mind. Your Asian woman has a lot going for her, Reg. For a start there are heaps and heaps of them. The whole of Asia is full of 'em and they're...I won't say they are cheap, I do not like that word, but they are within easy reach of the average Australian working man. They are like well designed cars: they take up less room, run on less fuel and yet once you get inside them you find there is just as much as there is in any of the larger models. Heaps of comfort and legroom to spare!

"They are cultured and artistic. They get into them tiny, weeny bikinis and dance all night long suspended from the ceiling in big birdcages. You should see the finger dancing! They are amazingly talented with their hands, Reg. And there is something very, very special about them. They all look the same, more or less. Some have different coloured dresses or bikinis on, that's how you tell 'em apart.

"Do you realize what that means for community relations, Reg? Everything would be different. Harmony would reign! You might, just for argument's sake, let us say that you might take home your mate's wife by mistake, or you might accidentally end up with her at their place because she looks just like your wife. And your mate won't mind at all because for all he knows he's been making the same mistake with your wife for the last six months. No fight, no big deal.

"But there's more, Reg, more. As you grow older, Reg, you'll notice that your Asian lass keeps much better than her Australian counterpart. She does not get wrinkles due to her diet of rice and fish. Her breasts - pardon me, Reg, but men must mention these things to each other from time to time - are smaller on the whole and stay firmer longer. And if you like great, big, pendulous Mombasa's why then there's always silicon to fall back on! Reg, think about it! Your little Asian girl has small, exquisite, agile hands, black hair, a tight, red, elastic mouth, an arching back curving down to the cutest little..."

"The water's boiling, Uncle Vern," I said.

"Get more water, Reg," said Uncle Vern handing me the bucket, "We're gonna cook her goose."

He followed me as I went to the tap.

"The way the white woman is going is it any wonder that Australian men are turning elsewhere more and more these days for their basic human needs? Why are the news stands full of pornography now? Magazines! Feminism! Twenty years ago you never saw anything like it! Sexual liberation! Huh!"

He spat on his own fridge in disgust.

"And the videos. Now don't get me wrong, Reg, I like art movies and magazines as much as the next man. But there is one thing seriously wrong with them.

They fill women with unreasonable expectations!
They are watching the movies and reading the
magazines and now they're full of ridiculous
demands.

"The sex isn't enough! They want this benefit and they
want that benefit, they want the chair pulled out and
the door opened and they want equal pay, they want
a new dress and you've got to protect 'em from abuse,
give 'em housekeeping money, give 'em a job ahead
of a man! They've got dishwashing machines and
clotheswashing machines and they're cooking with
gas and still they can't be relied on to have the dinner
steaming on the table on time after work! They're all
at committee meetings all about nothing. And what
do they do? Nothing! You can't get a woman to bend
over these days, not even to tie up her shoelace...Bless
me if your Auntie Mona doesn't sit down in an
armchair to put her shoes on! I mean! If they can not
stand the heat then they want to get right out of the
kitchen and move on over for someone who can!"

"Joe Blake was right. When his wife left was it the end
of the world? No. Did he crawl up a drainpipe and
die? No way! Did he go running after her with a sob
in his voice like some pathetic imitation of Hank
Williams? Did he drown his sorrows? No! No way!
No, he celebrated. He said, 'You little beauty! ' He left
the butcher shop in Bendoc in the care of old Birko
and he went to Manilla in search of a new bride.

"And did he get one? My bloody oath he got one. And she was beautiful! Far too good for him, as he often said himself. When he brought her back you shoulda seen all them young fellas lookin' after her, thinkin, 'Geee! ' But he didn't care and he was right. Joe was a man's man. His stomach was all paid for and he could drink with the best of them and he never backed down from nothing.

"And she, the reason for his manly confidence, she was polite, demure, delicate as the perfume of chrysanthemums. Joe's fibro-cement home by the mill was transformed by her cultured hand into an absolute palace of comfort and pleasure. She learned to cook chops with peas and potatoes and every night it was steaming on the table when he came home from work and she even took the top off his stubby for him in a way which he frankly found a bit embarrassing especially when they had the company of men of the world who had been to Manilla and who thought that she had picked up this habit from working in one of them bars.

"He got his conjugal necessities when he felt like them. There was definitely none of that headache bulldust that you get around here, I mean in this district that I have heard about. And when he wasn't up to it because he had been working too hard or his gout was playing up then that was not the cause of some major domestic dispute.

"All this, and yet do you know what, Reg?"

"What, Uncle Vern?"

"She didn't even like him. We could tell by the look in her eyes when he tried to kiss her on the lips at the pub, by the way she never seemed to enjoy the games of leapfrog and the way she squirmed when he tried to show some of the blokes...how's that water going, Reg?"

"Good, Uncle Vern!"

"Well, here, go and get another bucket. I think we'll get rid of that blasted peacock of hers. I'm gonna enjoy plucking that pea-headed, fancy-arsed barking bastard! Joe Blake's Asian bride, we knew she didn't love him. Joe confided in Polo that she had said that he, Joe, was masterful in his performance of the husband's office, but we knew better. We all knew and many of us - this was before I married your Auntie Mona - we would have been willing to help her out of her predicament but she wouldn't be in it. She was fearful faithful, I'm afraid. That was the only problem Joe had, really. The house started to fill up with pictures of Jesus and Mary. Joe even went to church a few times though there was nothing on but the service.

"She hated him, frankly, but she served him hand and foot. If he had to go anywhere, she drove him. She made the bed and faithfully helped to wreck it. She caddied for him at the golf club and she dived for his balls at the water trap and polished them after each round, and drove him home after the nineteenth hole.

"And we'd see him driving around in the passenger seat getting skinnier and skinner until he died. He'd drive around and sorta smile at us as if he knew how jealous some of them blokes were. And we'd look at him fading to a skeleton before our very eyes. Of course, there were all those stories about how she poisoned him but there was a post mortem and she was cleared of all suspicion although there are things like curare from South America which do not show up in autopsies, but anyway she did something very strange.

"Did she take the money and run off with some young buck? No. No, she stayed in the house all the time only venturing out to go to the shop and the cemetery. Yes, she went to the cemetery every day. For five years after he died she would get flowers from her garden every day and take them to old Joe's grave. Now that is what I call faithful. Grateful. Loyal. Respectful of the Lord and Master. These Asian women understand the meaning of the word servile. Absolutely blind, raving, naked in a glass bottomed boat mad Reg! Women are mad and the only choice a man has in this world if he is to avoid an early death from lockjaw of the wrist is what particular kind of madness he wants. And the Asian variety is not bad as they go. There is only one problem with it."

"What's wrong with slopes, exactly, Uncle Vern?" I asked, foolishly.

My Uncle looked at me as if there was something seriously wrong.

"Reginald you worry me. Sometimes I think you are rising to the station of manhood as surely as the sun rises over the mountains in the morning but there are other times when you are as remote from the real world as the stars. The problem with them, as if it needs to be spelled out for you, Reg, is that they are SLANTS! SLOPES! CHOWS! CHINKS! CHINGS! CHONGS! NIPS! GOOKS! JAPS! SLITTY-EYED YELLER PERILS! THEY ARE CHING CHONG CHINAMEN!"

"What's wrong with that Uncle Vern?"

I should have known better than to ask. My Uncle took a deep breath. A baleful look came over him. His veins stood up and throbbed violently and then he blew up.

"They are devil worshippers! They eat snakes and dogs! They munch on foul pickled weeds and sea slugs! They do not know knives and forks! They run their businesses examining the entrails of chickens! They smell. Endangered species - the mighty rhino and the mystic tiger - are vanishing from the earth so the sex mad Chinaman can get it up. They roam in gangs and work for nothing and live ten to a room and make millions of dollars that they send back to China for boat building! They sneak in our back door with their triads and defy our laws and smoke opium and gamble like fiends.

"But above all else, Reg, they multiply! They are worse than the rabbit! Reginald, you twerp! Just think of the multiplication! There are thousands millions of 'em already! They get a toehold in here and they will take over! The whole lot, lock, stock and barrel! We're just keeping it warm for 'em!

"Joe Blake's old wife was reduced to penury. Fair enough! But Joe, poor old Joe! He was not a saint I grant you that. But when he lay there gasping his last in his deathbed he was adrift in a sea of yeller! It was nightmare! She had brought the whole family out, fifty-three of 'em and they watched over him in his deathbed like vultures. Did he deserve that? Not one of his old mates was there to see him off, Reg! They couldn't get in! I had to call out from the verandah. 'I'll come back tomorrow when you're not so busy, Joe.' I don't even know if he heard me. I could just hear his weak, cancerous voice say ' No-more. No more, please. No more combination soup!'"

Uncle Vern so lost his composure that he threw a full stubby out the back door. It exploded against the slaughterhouse wall.

"Now see what they've made me do! Beware, Reg! You are targeted! They want to mate with us and dilute our blood. It's hard Reg. The white woman is ultimately to blame! In some ways I wish all women were slopes, Reg, but then before you could say 'Phuket Fat Dong' we'd all be slopes and our kids and the whole world would become slitty-eyed. Why did he have to marry her? You marry one, Reg, and all your children will be slanty and so will all their progeny from here to Armageddon. The white man will be finished. It's happening. Just look around. The two Brown boys, they married slopes. Their sister married that chink professor of chook guts - they don't visit us. They keep apart and yet they multiply. My God how they can multiply! In Manilla you should have seen 'em. Three, four, five, six girls come out of nowhere and they speak really good English. ' Hurro, Big Boy! ' they say. And you say, 'G'day, I'm an Australian! ' and they know exactly what you're on about. ' I get my rittoo sister! ' they say, 'or you want my rittoo brother? '

Uncle Vern's mind had slipped its mooring again. He thought he was in Manilla. He was foaming at the mouth and fumbling with his belt and he said to me,"

Aren't ya gonna open me another beer with ya thing, Darling? "

I hit him on the back of the head with the shovel.

He lay on the ground twitching. A strange feeling of well being came over me.

"Are you ok, Uncle Vern?" I asked.

"Thanks, son, I needed that," he said, "them slopes really get me going."

Good old Uncle Vern. He had about him a stoical quality that one could but admire.

"Uncle Vern?" I said.

"Yes, Reginald," he said mildly as he relaxed on the dirt floor.

"Is it true you're part Italian?"

"Who told you that?" he demanded angrily, springing to his feet.

"Auntie Mona may have mentioned it," I said, for I could but tell the truth.

"What! Mona! Mona! Mona get out here at once! I want a word with you!"

It gave me little pleasure hearing my Aunt and Uncle fighting and arguing, but a little pleasure was better than none, especially when I was on holidays at 'The Breakaways'.

 An Uncle Vern Story: Unfit for Human Consumption

DOCTOR WHO AND THE DARLINGS

a tale from the frontiers of science

An Uncle Vern Story: Wrong Way Go Back

Who. The mere mention of the name was an awesome thing. Dr Who, the mechanic from Wallabong, was six foot five if he was an inch, sixty inches around his chest, bald, ruddy and hale with a virile white moustache, hands like flanks of pork and even in his mid-sixties he was capable of throwing a full forty-four back onto a truck if he didn't like the way the driver said 'hello'.

But even more impressive than his physique was his intellect. Behind his glittering, steel spectacles and cruel blue eyes there lurked a brain as powerful as a sperm whale and more agile than a young slug in spring.

He was an inventor, a miner, a former merchant seaman, a student of geology and geography and the owner of a remarkable library of books that told you how to do everything from making perfumes and tactical nuclear devices to caponizing roosters and unlocking the secrets of the great pyramids of ancient Egypt. Behind his Wallabong garage he had a vast yard full of machinery: a gravel crusher, several trucks, a crane, lathes, welding gear, a bathoscope, lumber by the cubic metre, a gantry, a tractor, winches, a container full of nuts and bolts, old juke boxes, a half-built steel yacht, a blast furnace, a dismantled Fokker Friendship, a combine harvester, a bench saw and a fast breeder reactor he had made out of an old bain-marie, a microwave oven and Polo's old potato peeler and chipper, among other things. They called him Doctor Who because he could do anything.

Doctor Who was friendly with Uncle Vern from time to time. The news that he was coming was the cause of great excitement at the Breakaways, which is what Uncle Vern and Auntie Mona's farm was called on account of the great banks that were always breaking away and falling into the river.

Uncle Vern was soaking his hands in a bucket of lukewarm sump oil. He did this to impress the Doctor, to make him think that he, Vern, had been working hard.

Dr. Who's old Ford Canada with the crane on the back chugged inexorably up the hill. Sitting on the tray was a large black box. Uncle Vern wiped his hands vigorously on his overalls and said,

"Reginald, you are about to witness a momentous event. Dr. Who has invented a machine that will revolutionize human life as we know it on this planet. Do not tell your Auntie Mona this just yet, Reg, we do not want to upset her unduly, but here, today, here on this farm, the woman will be made redundant!"

"What!" I exclaimed.

"Yes, Reg," said Uncle Vern, "today we make history. And the Doctor has chosen me to be his test pilot!"

I was glad Auntie Mona was safely away in Daytrap, having a cappuccino at Polo's cafe.

The airhorn announced the approach of the great man as the big rig swung alongside the corral, guided by the doctor's brawny forearms. The airbrakes hissed, he cut the motor and leapt from the cabin in his hobnailed boots and dungarees positively bristling with good health and white chest hair.

"How're they hanging, Vern?" he said by way of a greeting. "Oh, hello, Reg, are you here on holidays? It's a hard life, eh?"

"Howdy Doc," said Uncle Vern.

The Doctor looked down at Vern's hands.

"What have you been doing to get in a state like that?" he asked.

"Just potterin' around," said Uncle Vern.

"I cannot believe this man," said Doctor Who to me. "I have never, ever in my entire life met a man who works as hard as your Uncle Vern. Every day he is up at the crack of Mona, going for it, aren't ya, Vern?"

It was a joke. The two men laughed loudly and it was not necessary for me to speak.

"Where do ya want it, Vern?" asked Dr Who lewdly.

""Behind the toolshed!" said Uncle Vern lewdly, and they both laughed loudly again. It was another joke.

Dr Who drove to the back of the toolshed while we walked. When we got there he had lowered the strange box to the ground. Uncle Vern and I loosed the dogs and let the chains fall.

The box was over six feet high and had recently been painted a glossy black. Beneath the new paint one could discern the embossed word 'Portaloo'.

"What's that, Doctor?" I asked.

"That, Reg," said Doctor Who proudly, "is the most advanced pleasure machine ever invented in the history of man. It is a Darling. The first Darling. Darling Mark II is already under construction and will incorporate the design changes which your Uncle's test run will indicate today."

"That's right!" said Uncle Vern.

"But what does it do?" I asked.

"I am not sure what it does at the moment," said the Doctor, "that's why we need Vern. But when it is finished it will do everything a man could want and much, much more. Eventually they will be fitted with incubator units that will raise the male foetuses to age fourteen when they will be old enough to go out and earn enough money to buy their own Darlings. There will be dish and clothes washing attachments and a computer for working out the household accounts with a modem for ordering the beer and groceries."

"Do you get inside it?" I asked.

"Questions!" declared Uncle Vern in a disgusted tone. "I have never known a boy to ask so many fool questions!"

"No, no, Vern. Leave the boy. He is right to ask questions. Inside this box, Reg, is everything that goes in and out, that tickles, slithers, scrapes, rubs, licks, sucks, spanks and slurps. It is based on the old sensory deprivation experiments, only in reverse. Instead of feeling nothing for hours on end, this machine will make a man feel everything all at once!"

No one spoke for a moment. The concept was staggering. Uncle Vern took out his hip flask and emptied it into his mouth, swilled it around so that it got into all his caries and sterilized his mouth ulcers, swallowed it and belched while saying my full name, a trick that had amused me when I was small. I must have been frowning, for he said,

"Cheer up, Reg! We're all going to be famous!"

It occurred to me for the first time that he might be killed in this wild adventure. I felt better and smiled back at him.

"That's it, Reg. Nothing's going to go wrong. The Doc's a genius!" He paused. "Well, I'd better get ready," he said at last and headed off to the toolshed.

Like Uncle Vern, Dr Who was a great yarner, but his style was very different, and, to my mind, preferable. For one thing, he did not always talk about the same business. He might suddenly launch into any subject on earth from embroidery to earth moving. His thought, like that of Uncle Vern, was provocative, but it was concise, without Uncle Vern's fancy twirls and trim. The Doctor would cut a topic from the herd, throw it, tie it, brand it and let it go before you even knew what it was. As soon as Uncle Vern left he said,

"Mah Jong. I used to play Mah Jong with my Uncle Jack from Rhodesia. He had a set made of vegetable ivory. It comes from a big tree with a fruit about the size and shape of an orange, but inside it is a large nut like a quandong and it is so hard that it can only be cut by a normal person with a diamond drill. Uncle

Jack made his with a three inch nail and eight thousand Swiss Army knives. He came to visit us once and when he got off the boat in Brisbane he had a wooden bicycle. The whole thing was made of wood, even the chain and the bell. It was a work of art and he had made it with his own hands, for me. It was my present. And do you know what my father did?"

I was about to say 'no' when I saw Uncle Vern emerge from the toolshed. He looked a sight in a wetsuit he had fashioned himself from Gladwrap with his typical rustic ingenuity, and the diving mask, snorkel and ever-ready gumboots.

"My father picked it up and smashed it on the ground and then he stomped on it. 'This boy is not allowed to have presents!' he said. That was my father."

"I never knew my father," said Uncle Vern rather forlornly through his snorkel.

"Quite right, that's the way it should be," said Dr Who. "It is a father's duty to leave home and spare his children the misery of having to live with him. I wish I never knew my...my Godfather Dick! What on earth is that?"

"A homemade flying suit," said Uncle Vern, somewhat defensively.

"Get it off!" ordered the Doctor. "You must go naked into the Darling. Just like the shower."

Uncle Vern was crestfallen.

"I wear a raincoat in the shower," he grumbled, but a stern look persuaded him that he had to change.

"No looking!" said Uncle Vern as he trudged back to the toolshed.

"You're not getting windy, are you Vern?" cajoled Dr Who.

Uncle Vern growled.

Dr Who attached a bit of hydraulic hose to a tap at the bottom of the forty-four on his truck and attached the other end to a large nipple on the Darling. He spoke as he worked.

"Take Tibet. All those priests and monks, thousands and thousands of 'em taking food from the mouths of the poor people, building great, big, useless monasteries and lamasseries and they produce nothing but prayers all day long. They flay people and make baskets of their hides. It is no better than medieval serfdom!"

"That's true, Doctor," I said, "but at least they don't have politicians and bureaucrats."

Doctor Who thought about this briefly and said,

"That's very good, Reg. Very true. Now, Reg, you needn't look when he comes out. It's not a pretty sight. But I must give him his final physical and fit him into her," said the Doctor, referring to the Darling. He called loudly to Uncle Vern,

"Remember you must come rampant, Vern, rampant!"

Uncle Vern coughed from behind the toolshed door and said, rather unconvincingly, "I'm ready."

The Doctor turned to see a naked, roaring, arm-waving Uncle Vern.

"Not that kind of rampant, Vern," said the Doctor, tiredly.

There was a moment of puzzled silence. In the corner of my eye I saw the Doctor make an aggressive gesture with his forearm but I was unfamiliar with its meaning.

"Oh," said Uncle Vern.

Moments later there came from the toolshed a vigorous rustling sound as of magazine pages being rapidly turned with one hand and a loud, stropping noise. After a tense few minutes the Doctor took a hip flask from his truck. I heard Uncle Vern's naked feet run to the Darling. Then Doctor who said, "Wait!" then, "Good!" and "Take this!" There was the unmistakable sound of alcohol disappearing into Uncle Vern. The Doctor gave terse instructions.

"Legs in there. Not there, there. That's it. When did you last have a shower, Vern? Now put that in there. You do it. I can't touch it it would compromise the integrity of the experiment. It's pre-heated. Tight? It'll loosen up once she gets going. It won't hurt once you get it in. Give me that picture. You right? Ok. Arms. Good. Head. OK. Under no circumstances remove the mask. You can communicate with us through the microphone in it."

Dr Who slammed shut the Darling's manhole. He ran to the truck, calling to me as he went.

"Quick, Reg, fasten those chains, there's no time to lose. He connected the crane to the Darling's ring, then ran to the forty-four and began operating the hand pump. Uncle Vern's voice crackled out over the intercom.

"What's that? What's happening?"

"Relax, Vern," said the Doctor. "That is the magic ingredient, Spermax. I invented it myself. It is made from pure sump oil and agar agar powder. It will do wonders for your complexion and it has no permanent side-effects. Are you still rampant?"

"Yes," said Uncle Vern.

The Doctor stopped pumping and began to operate the crane.

The crane turned and as it gathered speed the Darling slowly rose to the horizontal and began to make a noise like a router.

Once again Uncle Vern's quavering voice crackled out through the intercom.

"Help! Help! Let me out! Doctor! Reg! Mona! Help!"

"Turn that thing down!" ordered the Doctor. "He complains! You pay a dollar for a ride like that at the show!"

I was not sure what to do. The Doctor took the microphone.

"Vern. This is the Doctor. Relax, Vern. At the moment you will be feeling like a milkshake…"

Uncle Vern's voice gurgled back

"But I don't like milkshakes…"

"That's not what I mean, Vern. Stay with it. You will begin to feel better when you reach Mach 2 in about eighteen seconds."

The only reply was a series of appalling animal-like sounds. I felt deathly ill just listening to them. As I looked at the Doctor I could tell that he was also feeling the strain of listening to the inhuman noise. The cattle were bellowing in panic. Flaps the dog ran under the house. The air began to fill with crows and other carrion eating birds, and they circled high above us cawing hideously.

But then a miraculous transformation took place. Out of the bestial cacophony coming from the intercom a single sound was gradually woven, an eerie, visceral, moaning sound such as powerstations might make if they could know ecstasy. The cows' panic turned to an agony of desire. Desmond the bull threw himself desperately against the electric fence that kept him from them. Birds dropped from the sky. Flaps whined piteously. I covered my ears. Dr Who beamed.

"It works, Reg, it works! Don't be disgusted, Reg, it may be foul, but it is only nature."

He took my hands and started dancing. Just as I began to worry I was saved by a loud 'PING'.

Silence descended on everything. Moments later there was a loud crash as the Darling flew into the blackberries.

"Metal fatigue. Good old metal fatigue," said Dr Who, shaking he head. He dropped the broken link.

"Do you think he's all right?" I asked.

"I am afraid there is nothing on earth that could seriously harm your Uncle," said Doctor Who, as he slipped the dozer into gear and snigged the Darling out of the brambles.

"Stand back, Reg!" he said to me as he prepared to open the Darling's manhole. "We are in unknown territory."

We stood back together as the black, Spermax-covered form of Uncle Vern unsteadily clambered from the Darling and stepped gingerly onto terra firma.

"How was it, Vern?" asked the Doctor.

Uncle Vern said just one word before he collapsed in a black pool among the bramble canes.

"Fantastic!"

While we waited for the ambulance, Dr Who loaded the Darling back onto his truck.

"Boy children," he said, "should have their penises cut off at birth. By law. You know why? Because it costs them more money than all the other parts of their bodies put together!"

He seemed callously unconcerned about Uncle Vern's condition. He mounted his cabin.

"Reg!" he called.

He threw a metal frame to me.

"When Vern gets. out of the hospital give him this. It's his payment for being a test pilot."

The frame was oval in shape and about the size of a football with spring clips and two padlocks. I put it in the toolshed for safekeeping.

Six weeks later when Uncle Vern returned from the hospital he was mightily pleased to see what the Doctor had left him.

"The doctor's mind reaches into the past as well as the future, Reg," he said. "Though I fear the world is not yet ready for his Darlings, it is high time this little fellow was rehabilitated. For two hundred years it has lain in undeserved neglect."

"What is it, Uncle Vern?" I asked.

"This, Reg, is a Nag's Bridle. It is for your Auntie Mona when she needs it. We may not yet be able to do away with the woman, but at least we can rely on our ingenuity to win us some peace and quiet."

Of course I was sympathetic with Auntie Mona, knowing what she had to put up with; and yet the fact remained that she had married him of her own free will. It certainly was a mysterious world.

THE LOVED ONE

dishonour before & after death

An Uncle Vern Story: If Swallowed Seek Medical Advice

I was fast asleep in my room, dreaming that in the morning an armoured vehicle would come and careful men in uniform would tell me that my holiday was over and that I would have to go with them. My reverie was interrupted when I realized that the faint voice protesting my removal was in fact the small, whining, real-life voice of Uncle Vern.

I had often heard Uncle Vern call to Auntie Mona in the night. "Mona!" he would call. "Mo-ooonnaaa! I've got something for you!" Then he would try the door...but this was different.

"Mona."

The voice was plaintive.

"Mona!"

The voice was secretive.

"Mo-onnaa!!"

Uncle Vern sounded desperate. His voice was coming from the toilet. It seemed to indicate a degree of pain.

This was puzzling because as far as we knew Uncle Vern had not experienced pain for many years.

To be honest, I was afraid. I tiptoed to the master bedroom to rouse Auntie Mona. When I entered the room the bedlamp was on and I was shocked by what I saw. Despite the fact that Uncle Vern had often spoken of ancillary matters, I had never been privy to the sleeping habits of my Uncle and Aunt.

It looked at first as if my aunt had become a victim of the sort of crime one read about in the sort of magazines Uncle Vern liked to buy. The smell of chloroform abounded. Her face was covered with a mask and a weird apparatus encumbered her body. I gasped. I moved closer. It was only an aqualung. The chloroform smell was coming from wads of cotton stuffed up her nose. Her body was further protected by a full length raincoat done up to the neck. She wore a shower cap and she had her gumboots on. She was smiling so peacefully that I could not disturb her.

Reluctantly, I went to see what Uncle Vern's problem was.

"Mona! Mona! Mo-oonaa!!"

I approached with trepidation.

"Uncle Vern," I said, "Uncle Vern, it's me, Reggie!"

"Reginald, Reginald, help me! Come in, lad, and don't be squeamish. I think I am in pain!"

I entered the toilet. One of my Uncle's insect-like legs, horribly mis-shapen, had half-disappeared down the toilet bowl and appeared to be stuck in the 'S' bend. His face was noticeably greyer than normal. All of his clothes were lying on the wet floor. The room reeked of very bad wine. Uncle Vern held a silver bladder to his lips.

"Thank God it's you, Reg. I've run out of wine! Bring me a beer, son, make it a long neck. I can explain everything. My leg is broken in five places. Help me clean up so Auntie Mona doesn't notice. You know she doesn't approve of wine after dinner."

"Sure, Uncle Vern," I said, wondering how I was going to get him out of there. I grasped him under the armpits but he cried out.

"No! Reg, no! The pain! I can't feel pain! I mustn't! Doctor's orders! It would kill me. Don't even think about it. The toilet will have to be smashed. There's no other way. The beer, son, quickly!"

He seemed keen not to be moved. I brought the torpedo back and placed it just outside the toilet door, about a foot from his grasping, claw-like hand. He hardly had time to say "You bastard, Reg!" before his whole body slipped forward to enable him to grab the beer bottle and incidentally freeing his poor leg. He grunted as he guzzled at the life-enhancing beer.

The first job was to get him out of the bathroom. He was moaning and whimpering. I had to get some sort of anaesthetic. The alcohol was good in its way but we needed more. I ran to the bookshelf to get the folio of Modigliani. Uncle Vern, realizing what I was about, said,

"No, Reggie, we need something stronger. Bring Rubens."

I brought a blanket too, and, as he gazed at Rubens' bold and generous brush strokes, I placed the blanket beside him, rolled him onto it, tied the corners around his feet and lugged him into the lounge room. Then I rang the ambulance.

Taking a handful of newspapers from beside the fireplace I hurried to the bathroom and put them down to dry the floor.

"Reggie! Reggie!" Uncle Vern hissed to me, "Please, Reggie, beer!"

I took him another beer.

"I've rung the ambulance, Uncle Vern," I said, somewhat sheepishly.

"What?" said Uncle Vern. "You fool, Reggie. What do I need an ambulance for? Eh? What? Soft city people might seek medical attention for splinters and such-like but we in the bush are made of sterner stuff than that. I will be right as rain in the morning. Alls I need is a good night's sleep and a few aspro and if the leg is still playing up I can always jerry up a frame of fencing wire and star droppers. Jesus, Reg, do you think money grows on trees? Them Bairnsdale doctors are nothin' but a bunch of witch doctors. How many times they said I was gonna die? Eh? That's right, six. And they haven't been right yet. Horsedoctors! Huh! I wouldn't let 'em near my mule's reproductive system."

It was good to see his fighting spirit unimpaired. But then a spasm of pain shot through his entire body, convulsing it.

"Ah! Reg! Reg! Please, Reg! What's happening, son? Help me, Reg please."

This last appeal was so pathetic and heart wrenching that I was inclined to believe what he said next.

"This is it, Reg. I'm a goner. I am going to a far, far, better place, the grave. But you must stay here in Daytrap and I want you to do two things for me."

"Sure Uncle Vern," I said.

"Get me another beer, and never give your right name to them that don't know better."

I got him the beer. I was afraid that the effect of the beer would diminish, and that we may have to resport to even stronger measures. I had secreted his grandfather's old, lignum vitae collar-maker's mallet by the settee, just in case.

"Reg, I'm looking down the barrel, son."

"What can you see, Uncle Vern?"

"It's like a tunnel, Reg. There's a light at the end. It's only so tiny, but its getting bigger. It's a beautiful light, Reg. Really it is, I wish you could see it too."

Uncle Vern was looking up at Auntie Mona's treasured electric chandelier which he hated because it was always getting in the way. But then, his eyes were hardly open and who really knew what he was seeing?

"Reg, please Reg, I want to entrust you with something. My last will and testament, son, this is it. It's quite simple, really. Almost everything goes to my lovely Mona. Tell her I couldn't wait, son. Tell her I had to do what a man has to do. Tell her I died game, Reg.The house, the land, the toolshed and all the equipment, the dozer, they're all hers - but no other man is to use them, ever! Have you got that?"

"Yes, Uncle Vern," I said, reflecting that the house, the land and the dozer were Auntie Mona's anyway.

"I want you to have some of the personal effects, son. Auntie Mona can keep the Anal Intruder Kit - she may need it when I am gone, but you can have the library son, you can have the picture of The Girl From Ipanema, and the Nag's Bridle what Doctor Who gave me for being a test pilot, you can have the freezer in the toolshed and all the blackfish in it. You can have the tea tray I made out of matchsticks when I was a kid, and the stamp album, the X-ray specs, the bullworker and the Elvis clothes. Takes these things, son. You are the righful heir to the tradition, Reg. Please take these things and learn from them and let them be the light that guides you through this vale of tears, Reginald, son. And remember, Reg, I shall always..l...l...lu..lu..like you Reg, I'll always like you."

"Gee Uncle Vern," I said. It was kind of sad and yet highly ridiculous at the same time. "I don't know what to say." I said.

Uncle Vern slurped at his torpedo and dropped it onto the pouffe.

"Well try, 'Thanks Uncle Vern' for a start, you young ingrate!" said Uncle Vern.

I had heard of the intemperate behaviour of the dying and now I was seeing it. Under the circumstances it was forgivable. I had also heard of their incontinent behaviour, but I was used to Uncle Vern's little ways and this aspect of the dying process held no fears for me. It was all quite interesting, really.

"Reggie," said Uncle Vern, as he opened his new beer, "come closer son, there is something else I have to tell you. There is one story so terrible that until now I could not bring myself to tell you, but the time has come and if it is not to be lost forever then I must be relieved of its burden now. This is a dreadful tale but I tell it for your benefit, son. Keep the knowledge of what I am about to tell you and no matter how dark your days become you will always be able to reflect upon the fate of Cyril and his loved one and you will know that you have reason to rejoice because things can always get worse as this story shows."

His eyes glazed over and his gnarled paw reached up to grasp me blindly by the wrist as he began to tell his tale.

"Those stories Reg, about Cyril, and his tendencies, are true. We, his old friends and family, knew that he wouldn't hurt a fly. We knew Cyril. But it is true that he was asked to leave the district. That alone near killed him, Reg. His heart and soul were in this country. Heart and soul. Ripped out of him. They said go. Take the cun and the tree out of the country and what have you got left? Nothing! And that's what Cyril had when they showed him the road out of town.

"The road went two ways and that puzzled him at first but then he realized that it didn't matter which way he went as long as he went, so he went anyway. He wandered for years. Up and down and round about the wallaby track and back o' beyond the black stump. He saw more of the country than anyone from this district ever did, all because of his exile. He was brave about it. He kept going, looking for work at farms and in towns, keeping to himself, sleeping rough, moving, moving, always moving, dogged by the brand of shame, doing good wherever he could. Helping widows and spinsters and small children whenever possible. Chopping firewood, milking cows, giving haircuts, whatever came to hand.

"It was a fearsome lonely life. When you're living in a barn with the cows, even if you can manage the front to go to a dance smelling of Dencovit and Dynamic Lifter, with straws and other rubbish sticking to your Sunday Best, stuff attached to the ripple soles, even if you do manage to catch the eye of a comely, apple-cheeked country lass, you can't ask her to come back and spend the night with the livestock - not on the first date, anyway, I mean can you, Reg? It was hard. There may have been the odd one or two up against the back wall of the pub in nameless country towns, in the dark who can see what happens to who or who happens to what..."

Uncle Vern's voice trailed off. He seemed to reflect for a moment on his own troubles. He sucked again at his beer,

"Alice Springs! The dead heart! Real Australia! Cyril went there. He met a woman there. That's where his roving life nearly ended.

"Cyril's fortunes had been looking up. He had been made bar manager at the Riverside hotel. He was popular there, and he was making good money: fifteen quid a week all found. It was a good wicket.

"And yet his life remained empty. There was no shortage of women around. The main bar of the hotel was known fondly as the animal bar. It was a roaring place of good fellowship and hail-fellow-well-met all round. It was a melting pot. People from the bush and people from the town, oldsters and under-age drinkers mixed indiscriminately and no one knew no limits to nothing, that's the way Cyril described it.

"Every night he would see women, drunk women, loose women, footloose and fancy free tourist women who had come to the Territory for one reason and one reason only: to get among the real men in country where the ratio was better than the odds on a roughie.

"That was part of the trouble. Plenty of women seemed to like Cyril well enough but his duties required that he work in the bar until twelve when they closed and then he had to clean up.

"All night long he would work at the bar, joining in the jokes, slipping the odd free drink to his friends, and enjoying himself. He got plenty of offers, but by the time he got free the offers would always be taken up by someone else.

"He'd be in there cleaning up and he could hear as clear as anything the sounds of assignations being made outside the hotel, and from across the road in the river he heard the sounds of parties moving slowly this way and that towards their homes, laughing, drinking and canoodling noisily.

"But by the time he got out there, everything would be quiet and there would only be the croaking of dogs to keep him company.

"But as I said he had met this woman. One who seemed particularly interested in him. But every night she ended up going with someone else. She was young and keen, see, Reg, and just like Cinderella, she couldn't wait until after twelve o'clock.

"But then one, night she saved herself for him. It was his birthday and she surprised him.

"As usual after work, he went outside for his long and lonely poetic walk along the dry riverbed. He used to get to feeling pretty sorry for himself on these walks and he would take a bottle or two of the old Yellow Label along for company. This was back before they took it, and the Bundaberg pinktop, off the market - they always attack country people, Reg, have you noticed that? On this occasion, as it was his birthday, he took two.

"Anyhow he hadn't walked but three miles up and down stream when he saw his beloved lying under a bush, waiting for him. She had hidden there to surprise him, obviously, but she had fallen asleep in the long wait and there she was sleeping angelically.

"Her name was Morticia. Morticia Johnson. She wasn't pretty and she wasn't ugly, she was pretty ugly. Get it? Pretty ugly! Ha! Ha! It's a joke, son!"

I did my best to laugh. Uncle Vern was certainly putting a brave face on things, one had to admire that.

"Poor old Cyril said to her, 'Morticia! Morticia!' but she did not wake up. He knew she was a heavy drinker - he had been pouring the stuff into her for some time - so he was not surprised by this. He tried to revive her party spirit by giving her a little sip of the port but that did no good either.

"So, resigned to a quiet night, he thought, 'Ah well, I shall lie down here and keep her company. I shall keep the packs of marauding wild dogs away. Just friendly-like. So he lay down beside her and prepared for sleep.

"But sleep did not come. For Cyril was worried about his birthday. He had not received one card or present from anyone wishing to help him celebrate. The people in the bar were too busy getting drunk to be interested in his birthday. People, thought Cyril, were so superficial and callous. They didn't care about other people even enough to notice when it was their birthday. Alice Springs, Cyril decided was not a country town any more. Alice Springs was a city.

"And the only person who cared enough to wish him happy birthday was Morticia, his best friend. She had a heart of gold and had been his close personal friend and confidante for nearly a fortnight now: she alone cared and had waited all this time for him to knock off work. He almost regretted slipping the extra nips of vodka into the Orgasm he gave her just before stumps. If it hadn't been for that she might have been awake now and singing 'Happy Birthday' to him...and undoubtedly there would have been a birthday kiss to go with it.

"The big yellow moon came up over the riverbed like a drunken sailor with half his face caved in. By the sepulchral light of the desert moon he could see that Morticia was smiling in her sleep. He felt protective towards her. He thought to himself how disappointed she would be in the morning when she realized that she had not given him his birthday kiss. So he decided to give her the birthday kiss and tell her about it in the morning....aaaaaAAAgggGGGHHH!!"

"You OK, Uncle Vern?" I asked.

"Painkiller! Painkiller!" he gasped.

I handed him another bottle of Auntie Mona's Pimm's No. 1 Cup. He drank half of it and said,

"Is that all we've got left, Reg? I don't think I can make it, boy."

He broke an empty bottle over his own head and then used the jagged neck to make a gash on his chest. Gathering blood from the wound in a glass he mixed it with more Pimms and drank it.

"That's better," he said, with evident relief. "Cyril leaned over his close personal friend Morticia not realizing at first that powerful pheromones were acting on his mind. Do you know what pheromones are, Reg?"

"No, Uncle Vern," I said, and it was the truth.

"Pheromones are nature's way of saying to people, 'come an' get it!' The are natural perfumes released by the body unconsciously. Wise countrywomen do not use Chanel No. 5 or rubbish like that which is made from substances like panic-smegma cruelly extracted

from innocent tom cats while their faces are whipped
with barbed wire. It is a waste of time and money and
cruelty. No, a wise countrywoman, when she is on the
prowl, just puts a couple of fingers of nature's own
perfume behind her ear when she goes out for a walk
and lets the pheromones do the work for her."

"Gosh," I said.

"Yes, Reg, and when Cyril began to kiss Morticia he
had absolutely no intention of putting his tongue in
her mouth for instance, but her powerful pheromones,
operating even while she was asleep, made him do it.
So he did it. And it was good. Cyril kissed her without
inhibition in the dark, in the river, in the moonlight
and in the end passion took over completely. He
kissed her everywhere, mercilessly and when he was
ready, he possessed her."

"It was an incredible experience. Several hours later,
when Cyril was finished, as they lay back on the
grassy bank relaxing, Cyril told her of his dreams. He
was going to go back to Daytrap and reclaim his part
of the ancestral farm from his wicked stepbrothers
and there with the sweat of his brow and the strength
of his hands he was going to carve the best alfalfa
farm in the district out of virgin bush and he would
raise his sons to be men and his daughters if he had
any could be men too and he wanted her, Morticia, to
come with him. He wanted to take her away from all

that to be his bride in white and walk down the aisle with him and into the sunset happily for ever after, amen. Finally, he told her, he felt that his life had fallen into place and he now had everything he needed to wrench his share of contentment from this wretched life. Aagghh."

Uncle Vern winced as he sipped another life-affirming draught of blood and Pimms.

"It is a bitter, cruel world, Reg," said Uncle Vern. "A cruel and bitter world. 'Whaddaya think, Darl,' asked Cyril after he had told her of his idea. She did not even reply. He elbowed gently.

'Morticia, what do you think?' he said, fondly. She did not snuggle up to him and say 'Hmmmn?' She did not even snore. He shook her roughly by the shoulder, 'Do ya want to live happily ever after or not ya stupid slut?' he said, roughly, because he thought she was ignoring him. But still she did not respond.

"It was nearly dawn. In the steel light he saw that her skin had turned grey overnight. He took her by the hand and realized that she was no longer among the living. The passion and excitement of the night must have been too much for her heart condition, for now she was as stiff as, as...as stiff as stiff could be.

"It is times like these Reg, that test the mettle of a man. Cyril had seen everything melt into nothing before his very eyes in but a few seconds. Broken, cruelly broken-hearted, he knew that life must go on. Cyril had a remarkably low IQ - you know what an IQ is don't you Reg?

"Yes, Uncle Vern," I said.

"Well, Cyril's was remarkably low for a normal person, but he was not stupid. He went straight to the police station."

In the distance we heard the ambulance's siren wailing as it sped towards The Breakaways. Uncle Vern began to panic.

"Don't let them near me, Reg, don't let them doctors near me. I will allow myself to be touched by nurses only! Only nurses, do you hear me, Reg?"

"But Uncle Vern, what did Cyril do?" I asked.

"He was aware of his duty as a citizen and was always happy to help the police. He explained that he was out for his constitutional when he discovered the body of the woman under the bush. He did not fully explain his role in the matter, of course, as he knew that that would only lead to pointless questions and complications. He had never seen her before in his life except at the pub where he worked. The police agreed that it was a shocking thing to find the woman like that. Their initial investigations suggested that she had died of horror.

"Let this be a lesson to you Reg. Cyril might have been in big, big trouble if he had not been in the habit of wearing a condom, what with the DNA testing they do these days. He always wore a condom as I do. I've got mine on now, it is the first thing I put on in the morning. Boy scouts! Be prepared, dyb! dyb! dyb! Will dob! dob! dob!

"Several days later he heard on the grapevine that police tests had showed that Morticia had had sex with ten different men in the hours before she died, and that she had been dead at least twelve hours when they found her. Cyril wondered. Then he began to feel sick just thinking how close he had come to making a woman like that his wife. He went back on the road and continued his life of wandering."

The ambulance screeched to a halt on the gravel. The men in white had been there before and knew the way. They rushed in wearing gasmasks and without a word they snigged out Uncle Vern, gagged him, deftly tied him to a wheeled stretcher, tied the stretcher to the towbar and drove off again. It was amazingly quick and painless.

I cleaned up as best I could and went to bed pretending that I was a pygmy possum. I can't quite explain it, but somehow I was tiring of, not of life, but of being a human.

THE INTERSTELLAR SEXDRIVE

probably all lies

An Uncle Vern Story: HAZCHEM

Uncle Vern was an old cub from way back and he still shook hands with other old cubs the secret way. Holding pride of place on his five foot shelf of books, alongside Brunning's 'Australian Home Gardener', Corrie's 'Advanced Animal Husbandry' in ten volumes, Mrs Beeton, "More Joy" , and fourteen years of bound 'Playboy's (which Uncle Vern only read for the articles,) was the famous classic by Lord Baden-Powell, "Scouting for Boys" . We always took it with us when we went camping.

Despite the tedium of Uncle Vern's stumbling attempts to 'bond' with me, as Auntie Mona called it, notwithstanding my own devotion to the great indoors, camping was one of the few activities I engaged in during my visits to their farm that I sometimes enjoyed. There was a magic about clear country nights to which even I was prone.

Having paddled upstream in our kayaks we made camp on a grassy bluff overlooking the river. We were miles from civilization. The crickets and cicadas had quietened for the night. Above us the countless stars whirled on their majestic cartwheel as we silently contemplated the cosmos. Somewhere downstream a couple of swans honked.

There was a tremble in the timbre of Uncle Vern's catarrh-enhanced speaking voice that I had not noticed before. The bulky, crepe bandage that the doctor had put over his nose after removing the polyp made it slightly difficult for him to talk with his usual fluency, yet as his words began to unravel they did not fail to weave their old spell.

"Onkaperinga, Reg. Onkaperinga! That's the Aboriginal word for sky. The sky is a big blanket, Reg, a good but old wool blanket and it hangs over us everywhere. There is a world beyond it with a light and the stars we see are but the chinks of light coming from that other world, shining through tiny holes made in the blanket by the moths of time."

I was feeling tired already. The outdoors life affects me like that.

"There are times in a man's life, times of heightened awareness - you remember what happened to that bloke with the hippie girls that I told you about - that was a good example of what I mean - and on these occasions - are you listening, Reginald?"

"Yes, Uncle Vern," I said, but I was lying.

An Uncle Vern Story: HAZCHEM

"On these occasions a man gets right up close to the blanket and he can, by dint of superhuman effort, peek through the veil and into the other side, and do you know what he sees, Reg?"

"What, Uncle Vern?" I asked. One needed only a few phrases, really, to converse with Uncle Vern.

"You see the other half of a remote, sturdily built shack, lit by a hurricane lamp. There's a bed with an eiderdown and a fire, a wall covered with calenders from butchers and mechanics and on the outside of the delicately lace-frosted windows, a roaring blizzard. In the middle of the room there is a woman with rough, strong limbs, breasts that are firm and tangy like cheddar cheese and her chemise is pulled up over her head. She is Neanderthal, Reg! The dappled light of the dancing flames plays on the bush! The bush! The fire! The bush! The foosh! Fire! Fish!..Fire!...Fishfire! Fishfire! Help!..oh my God!..."

My Uncle seemed momentarily overcome by emotion.

"Look Uncle Vern, a shooting star," I cried, trying to change the subject.

"Oh, oh sorry, Reg," he said.

I looked at him quizzically but said nothing.

"But, Reg," he said at length, tiredly, "all this peaceful night sky, it is all a bitter illusion! Ask Dick Katz, if he'll talk about it."

As we sat in silence I tried desperately to go to sleep, for I knew, as sure as sheep are shorn, another story was coming. The stars throbbed and groaned above us, as if in expectation.

"They're out there, Reg," said Uncle Vern.

There was something eerie in the way he said this, as if he were actually afraid.

"What, Uncle Vern? Nocturnal snakes?" I asked.

"No, Reginald, who cares about snakes? They are far worse than mere snakes."

"Who are they Uncle Vern?" I had to ask.

"The aliens, Reg. The aliens that switched Dick Katz' eyes. You know Dick Katz, don't you?"

I remembered Dick Katz from Young Andrew's twenty-first birthday party at the hall. There had been five of us gathered around the firedrum that night if you included young Andrew, who was unconscious most of the time: myself, Vern, Dick Katz and Dick's dog, Darren Millane. I can recollect little of the evening except that every time I started to speak Dick said to me, "Who pressed your button?" or "Who crossed your wires?" or "Who pulled your chain?" or

"Who switched you on?" Later Dick treated me in a warm, comradely way in front of the men on the verandah of the Daytrap Hotel when he averred that we had drunk a whole keg of beer among us and he put his arm around my shoulders, hugging me in the manly, rural way that has gone out of fashion in most parts of the country and saying, repeatedly, "There were no poofters at that turn!" But I had only seen him a couple of times in the dark and did not know him well.

"Yes, Uncle Vern," I said.

"Well, you know how he's got one blue eye and one brown eye?"

"You mean two blue and one brown don't you Uncle Vern?"

"Don't be disgusting, Reg," said Uncle Vern. "His right eye is blue and his left eye is brown. But before the aliens got him it was the other way around. That's how we know for sure it happened."

He paused. "Well?" he asked.

"Well what, Uncle Vern?" I asked.

"Well aren't you gonna ask me what happened?"

"Sorry, Uncle Vern, I was breathless with anticipation."

"Oh, very good, Reg, well, I'll tell you."

He pulled deeply on his trusty shag and scratched himself vigorously before beginning.

"You know why people don't like Dick Katz?" Uncle Vern asked. "It is not because he starts arguments; it is not because he is loud-mouthed, abusive know-all, completely full of crap; it is not because he only talks about tyres and petrol and tax; it isn't because he is bald and ugly; it is not because he always wears overalls and reeks of Brut aftershave. No. It is none of these things. It is because there is a wanting about Dick Katz, a deep, and, to some people, a frightening wanting about him, an obvious wanting which is also subtle and can not be spoken of; and no one, least of all Dick, knows what it is that he is wanting. That's why people shy away from him."

Uncle Vern mused silently. I thought it best not to speak.

"Perhaps," he said at last, "perhaps that has something to do with what happened and perhaps not, but the fact remains, Reg, that Dick Katz saved this planet from certain annihilation by merciless and hideous aliens.

"It's funny I should say 'merciless', because Mercia was the name of Dick's late, beloved wife. At the time of the encounter with the aliens he had only recently

                    An Uncle Vern Story: HAZCHEM

been widowed. His dear, departed wife had been wheelchair- and bed-ridden for many long years and Dick had always been the model of the faithful, patient husband, always pushing her around flower shows and auctions when he wasn't out working to put bread on the table or doing the housework.

"But it was a trial. The real Dick, the Dick we all knew in the bar, was a total dingo, an utterly shameless dingo. But he suppressed all his natural and abundant joie de vive - that's French talk for Joy of Life, Reg - for the sake of his poor, dear wife's reputation. For a woman, Reg, reputation is her most precious possession. In fact a reputation is all many women have got between them and the wolf at the door. And Dick made that sacrifice for her, just as she had had to make some terrible sacrifices to him on the holy altar of their matrimony.

"But what about the aliens, Uncle Vern," I said.

"One night about ten years ago, soon after his poor wife had died, Dick was down in Lennie's paddocks, square baiting the river and brooding. While he was sitting there in the dark, all by himself, wondering whether to put on another jumper against the chill night air or whether to jump in the river and drown, his attention was arrested by a large, garishly lit thing hovering above the river not far away. At the same time as he saw this strange thing he began to hear heavenly voices singing to him. You know, like on TV variety shows when they have chiffon everywhere and a sylph flutters all round the stage and there's all strings and a big choir of female voices sings but what they sing isn't words, well, that's what it was like. Out of the laas and waahs and weeeyooos he started to hear his name being called. ' Diiick, Diiickie!' it sang, 'Weeeyee deyeeesire youhoowoohoo Diiick. Cuhuhuhum, cuhuhuhum tooooo uhuhuhus!'

"Dick, alone, cold, his life empty as a broken promise, was fair game for this sort of thing. The alien craft drifted about him, playing this music and displaying stroboscopic lights around it's girth that seemed to have a hypnotic effect. Even though he had no boat Dick, in a daze, grabbed his four remaining beers and walked across the river, following the strange starship. As he went he saw his faithful pooch, Darren Millane, fretting on the riverbank, with a puzzled look on his face. 'Hang Doggy!' he commanded.

"The UFO floated slowly over the dense bush, just above the trees. Dick followed like a man possessed, caring not that he tore his clothes and flesh on thorns and branches that he could not see in the dark. Having led him to a remote place it landed and a gangplank was lowered to the ground.

"Dick heard angelic voices calling on him to come aboard and have a good time and he walked into the

                    An Uncle Vern Story: HAZCHEM

clutches of the aliens like a zombie, with nothing but four beers for self-defence.

"When he got aboard the door slammed shut. In some part of his mind he had registered that the strange craft had some curiously familiar markings on it's hull. The letters" K.T.B. "became fixed in his memory despite the ordeal that was to follow.

"There was a thick fog inside the spaceship. Dick could see nothing at first. The voices kept singing the well-known song" The Girl From Ipanima "and he felt strangely warm. Suddenly he was sitting in a chair that he could not see and there were two lights before him. As his eyes became accustomed he began to make out the shapes of the alien beings

"There were hideous, and yet compelling. Dick could not keep his eyes off them. One, which turned out to be the male, was an oval shape. It's main feature was a large vertical mouth which had not one set of lips, as a human mouth has, but two sets of lips. It might have been anything from three to six feet high. Aside from the lips the only other recognizable feature Dick could make out was a thick coating of hair over the rest of the creature's body. It propelled itself by means of a subtle muscular action in the lower part of its mouth which ran along the ground. If you are thinking this creature was a bit like a slug, Reginald, you would be right because when it moved it left behind it a silver trail."

"Sounds disgusting, Uncle Vern." I said.

"That was Dick's feeling too," said Uncle Vern, "and yet he also found the hideous thing strangely attractive. It seemed to remind him of something.

"The female creature was even more bizarre. It's lower part, the means of locomotion - oddly quite different from the male - consisted of a couple of large ball-like objects and these supported the main body, a sort of trunk. The mouth of the female was at the top and was much smaller than that of the male.

"At first they tried to communicate with Dick by means of grunts, snorting and snuffling, but then they got the telepathic translator machine going and he was able to converse with them in perfectly clear English.

"'Hello Dick ' they said, 'You are aboard our intergalactic spacecruiser. Do not be alarmed. We are doctors. Everything will be all right. This will not take long. We only want to look at you.' Dick was suddenly seized by a levitation ray and suspended horizontally above the ground. The male creature removed his clothes by sucking them from his body. Dick's instinct was to protect himself but the ray held him fast. From the dim ceiling of the spacecraft a great big thing that looked like a dentist's Swiss army knife came down and probed him quickly and thoroughly, and then a mechanical voice crackled through the air.

"'Stand back! Stand back! Countdown to dismemberment commencing now! 100-99-98-97-96-95-94-93-92-miss a few - 2 - 1 - 0! Dismember! Dismember! Dismember!'

"As Tom's body fell apart, evil space laughter filled the alien craft. And yet his eyes kept seeing and his brain kept thinking. He would have given anything to lose consciousness but he could not.

"His eyeballs were floating in space. So were the rest of his body parts The air was highly charged with ionized particles. Dick had the queerest sensation that all his body parts had been dusted with sherbert. Blue flashes exploded silently around him as if he were being hounded by little green papparazzi. His liver banged into his brain. His stomach was naked and vomitting into the void. His left ear was as itchy as anything but he could not scratch it as his hands were busy trying to catch his other floating parts.

"Just as he thought he was going to go completely mad the metallic voice barked the brief command, 'Reconstitute!' and he was put back together again.

"Tom's initial relief turned to horror when he realized that they had put him back the wrong way. They had made a complete meal of it. His sex organs were now uselessly mounted on his shoulder blades. The hair from his head had swapped places with his buttock furze. His eyeballs were lying sightless in his scrotum, his testicles were lodged in his eye sockets, his sweetbreads were in his skull, his lips had swapped with his anus while his tongue and penis had confused their positions, as had his feet and hands. Imagine his horror at not being able to see these things but only feel them with his feet.

"' I told you, Mi Kel, we should have had the thing serviced. You should have done this manually.' said the female space creature.

"' Nonsense, Wil-Ma! ' said Mi-Kel. ' It looks much better this way.'

"' Put it back together properly, Mi-Kel!' ordered Wil-Ma.

"' Do not worry, Wil-Ma,' said Mi-Kel. 'I will give it a squirt of ether in the infoducts and she will fire up real good!'

"There was a loud yet gentle 'Pffffft' sound and all Dick's parts were floating again, and again he was thrown together the wrong way. Eight, maybe ten times he underwent this ordeal, and throughout he was kept sane by one thought: 'Geez I'd love a beer!' he thought.

                    An Uncle Vern Story: HAZCHEM

"Finally the aliens got it right and Dick was put together almost as good as he had been before. Only the eyes had swapped places. The mechanical voice crackled out once more:

"'The earth creature is in good health. It appears to be bisexual, predominately female, with a morbidly enlarged concupiscence and of extremely limited intelligence. If this is the best this planet has to offer then conquest will be easy. Mating with this creature would not be difficult, but I would advise against it.'

"Though he was immobilized, Dick understood what was going on around him. The two aliens were talking in their grunt talk. They did not realize that Dick could now understand them. The male one was saying, 'I do not care, I will mate with it anyway.' The big, hairy form of the male alien began to slither towards Dick who was still held fast by the paralysing ray.

"'Turn on the Muzak,' the creature commanded.

The well-known song 'The Girl From Ipanima' was playing far faster than was normal. The male creature slithered this way and that around Dick as if trying to make up its mind about something. As it passed its hairs brushed Dick and he noticed in mute terror that it had begun salivating violently. The air was thick with its musty odour. It was a sticky situation. And it was beginning to affect his mind. For each time the creature went around him it looked more and more human. Dick felt an alien excitement growing within him, against his will. A lesser man might have cracked, but not Dick Katz. He fought it with all his might. Dick was determined to show these aliens what an earth man was made of! But what could he do?

"But then the male creature, rapidly going into a frenzy, began to argue with the female one.

"'Go on Wil-Ma, turn off the ray!'

"'No, Mi Kel, it could be dangerous you must not turn it off !'"

"'But Wil Ma, it is much better when they struggle. I hate doing it with a log. I will have my way!'

"The creature was almost upon him, its great, slavering lips writhing in expectation. It seemed about to swallow him whole.

"The ray was turned off. Now was Dick's chance. Though it was dark and he hardly knew what he was doing he went into a frenzy and attacked everything in sight. He picked up objects and threw them at the space things. He destroyed a console of flashing lights, he put his foot through a transponder. Then, crucially, he found his beers. One he threw against the wall. It exploded in a maelstrom of foam and glass, stunning and alarming the aliens. Thinking instinctively, he shook another stubby ripped the top off it and holding his thumb partly over the neck sprayed them with beer. The aliens were afraid of beer. Dick sprayed them mercilessly.

"The space things panicked at the sight of such fury. They tried to turn their rays on but they would not work. The female one was complaining to the male: 'I told you not to turn off the paralyser ray. But oh no, doing it with a log isn't good enough for you! In three hundred galaxies I have not seen a more disgusting creature! Now look at the mess it is making! It has made three separate messes on the floor already. Get it out of here! And get its clothes out too!'

"' You are right, Wil Ma! We must leave this planet! These earthlings are too mighty for us! We must never come here again!'"

"Soon after this Dick found himself outside the spaceship, naked and shivering, with his clothes in a heap beside him. He dressed as best he could in the dark and staggered blindly through the bush towards home and civilization.

"In the morning he was found curled up like a baby on the verandah of the hotel. His wild story was believed by no one at first but because he was so insistent some of us went with him to look for the site of these incidents. He felt sure that there must be some signs left of the aliens' visit. He insisted the spacecraft had the letters 'K T B' written on the side, though none of us, Dick included, could imagine why that would be. And yet, there was something familiar about it.

"All the way Dick was distraught. He was desperate not to be taken for a crank. I remember him beggin' me like a child, Reg. ' Please, Vern, please, I am telling the truth, you've got to believe me Vern. The hairy, oval shaped ones with the big lips were the males...' It was pretty pathetic, Reg, I don't mind telling you.

"But then we seen it. There was a great, big 10,000 gallon concrete tank in the middle of the bush, all dirty and overgrown and looking like it had been there since the flood and the words 'Kerton's Tanks, Bairnsdale' were written on the side. It didn't look like a spacecraft, but on the other hand what was it doing way out there in the bush, far from any house? It could have been washed there in a flood, but no one could remember such an incident... the more likely possibility was that it could also have been a clever ruse left behind by aliens wishing to cover their tracks, alien creatures who thought earth people were stupid or somethin', and that they could easily discredit their conqueror, Dick Katz!" said Uncle Vern contemptuously.

He paused significantly. The moon was just starting to come up between the cleft formed by two mountains. It was big, and yellow.

"Not all of us believed him even after we had seen the tank, Reg. We all climbed inside to see if there was any other evidence. Alls we could find was two wombats killed recently by an apparently superhuman force, and a broken stubby.

"I looked Dick square in the eye. 'Are you tellin' us the truth, Dick,' I asked.

"' Yes,' said Dick."

"' Really? ' I said and then I realized, 'My God!' I cried, 'Dick they've switched your eyes around. '

"The men all gathered round and looked on, amazed, as they realized what I had said was true. Dick's eyes had been switched.

"No one knew what to say. No one wanted to speak. We have hardly ever spoken of it since.

"We were about to turn back when Dick remembered his net. So we went with him and when we got there we found the two hugest mullaway you ever saw caught in that net. That famous picture of Dick in between the two fish was taken later that day and is the first picture ever taken after his eyes were switched by the aliens."

"Gee, that's an amazing story, Uncle Vern," I said.

"I only hope it doesn't give you bad dreams, Reg. Goodnight son."

"Goodnight Uncle Vern," I said, snapping closed the padlock on my sleeping bag and falling at once into the arms of Morpheus.

                                   An Uncle Vern Story: HAZCHEM

BULL'S WEDDING

a bushy tale

An Uncle Vern Story: Pedestrians Watch Your Step!

One morning Uncle Vern went to the fridge in his toolshed to get a stubby for breakfast and found to his horror that he was reduced to his last half dozen. He was meant to be crotching the sheep that day, and crotching, as is well known in rural circles, is very thirsty work.

"Jeez, Reg, what am I gonna do?" he moaned.

"Don't worry, Vern, don't worry! Vern, stay cool," he said to himself, adding for my benefit, "Reg I mustn't worry because that only aggravates the thirst. Stoically he put his sixpack under his arm, took his rusty handshears from their nail and headed off after his sheep, calling to me as he went.

"Fill the small Esky with ice, Reg, and get me some thin straws from the house. Set the alarm clock for nine forty-five. We'll have to eke it out!"

As the endless numbers of sheep passed through Uncle Vern's rough, practised hands, I watched the beads of sweat constantly forming all over his craggy face. They gathered into large droplets on the end of his nose where they hung for what seemed like an eternity before jumping off into the void. After every four or five drops fell Uncle Vern would ask me,

"Reg, what's the time?"

"Seven fifty-three, Uncle Vern," I would say, "Seven fifty-four and a half, seven fifty-six, Uncle Vern."

He would have a miserly sip of beer through a straw and get back to his work.

He was doing it hard, yet, until nine thirteen, he uttered not one murmur of complaint. Then, when I told him the time, he threw down his shears saying,

"It can't be! It can not be!"

He picked up his shears again and stared at them uncomprehendingly, he staggered out among the sheep, raising his arms despairingly in the bright, clear, cruel morning sky, and crying out with all his might,

"I HATE TIME!"

Then he fell in a heap among the gentle, unconcerned animals. I thought it best to let him have a lie down for a little while. As I waited for him I gazed at the grass. I could see myriad small creatures creeping and crawling hither and thither, waving their feelers around, dragging things, eating each other. There were so many creatures that it was like another world and I began to wonder whether Uncle Vern should really be lying face down on it. The little creatures might crawl up his nose or into his ears and then what would become of them?

Up in the sky a pair of ospreys soared and swooped and hung on the powerful currents of air that rose from the overheating land.

Then the alarm went. Uncle Vern struggled to his feet and I passed him a glistening, cold stubby of beer which he had previously overlooked in the bottom of the ice. With wordless gratitude he took the beer and began to run to his Tojo.

"Come on, Reg," he called cheerfully, "we don't want to be late!"

We sped into Daytrap. He was in an uncommonly good mood and suggested that we might as well take the rest of the day off. I was worried that this might lead to yet another story, but things did not work out that way as you shall see. Uncle Vern backed his ute up to the hotel to take aboard his load of beer. As we passed by the verandah we heard from within the sound of raised voices.

"Guts of a monkey!" shouted one.

"Mould!" shouted the other, even louder.

"Guts of a monkey! Be told!" yelled number one.

"Mould, you moron!" yelled the other, even louder.

"THE GUTS OF A FRIGGIN' MONKEY, I SAID!" screamed the first voice.

"MOULD, IDIOT! MOULD! MOULD! MOULD!" Screamed the second, even louder.

"WHERE WAS THE MOULD YA STUPID MOLL? IT WAS IN THE GUTS OF A FRIGGIN' MONKEY! QUIET! YOU DON'T KNOW WHAT A WILDMAN IS!" bellowed the first voice.

A door slammed and boots stomped along the verandah not far from us. Uncle Vern shot me a knowing, derisive look, and shook his head. I could not see who was on the verandah because of the thick hedge and the passionfruit vine that sprawled all over it. We heard a small grunt and an arc of fluid sailed gracefully through the air and struck Uncle Vern on his Stetson.

He took an alarmed step backwards and said, sternly and aggressively,

"Whaddaya think you're doin'?"

A red head with red hair, red freckles and red eyes poked over the hedge while the offending fluid continued to trickle through the pittosporum.

"Oh, jeez, sorry Vern, bro! Did I getcha man? I'll buy ya a beer! Nah, jeez! what am I sayin'? I'll buy yez a Jim Beam, that's worth at least a Jim Beam, and one for the young fella. Can't start 'em too young, eh?" rasped his much abused voice.

Then the strange little man came down the steps. His long, red hair was tied at the back with a bit of barbed wire. The air around him reeked of spirits and stale bile With his yellow teeth and all the red his head looked like it was on fire. He was wearing denim jeans and a fur-lined denim jacket over a red-checked shirt and oversized black biker's boots. Extending a hand bristling with lethal rings he grasped Uncle Vern's wrist, shook it, slid his hand into the thumb wrap shake, gave him the hooked fingers shake and finally applied a regular handshake with powergrip.

At first, not being used to this elaborate greeting, Uncle Vern began dodging on the spot and preparing to block or throw punches but finally he settled into the powergrip and the two men faced each other, squeezing as hard as they could without flinching.

Then Uncle Vern broke away crying "Finger!" The strange man released his grip and Vern held up 'Old Tickler', his crippled finger. The small man feinted a punch, Uncle Vern weaved away, dropped his left and threatened with a right. Jab, jab went the other.

"Vern! Mad Vern!"

An Uncle Vern Story: Pedestrians Watch Your Step!   97

"How're you, Bull?" said Uncle Vern, in a stern, manly, country way.

"Friggin' bewdiful, Vern!" said the Bull. "When are ya gonna come out to the farm and help us sink a few, Vern? Haven't seen you for ages, man!"

"Too much work to do, Bull," said Uncle Vern, rather pointedly. "We gotta go, man! Time is tight!" said Uncle Vern, hurrying away "See ya!"

"Dig ya, baby!" said the Bull.

As we turned from the pub Uncle Vern muttered to me,

"Bloody stupid feral. Give it a wide berth, son, a wide berth."

We were crossing the road in an unhurried rural way when we were startled by a roar. Tyres squealed and smoke billowed as a supercharged V8 Ford Fairlane careened around the corner. The woman driver yelled an obscenity and made a one-fingered gesture at the hotel.

The flabbergasted Bull, jigger in hand, appeared on the verandah again.

"BITCH!" he yelled. "COME BACK HERE, YOU BITCH! THAT'S MY CAR!"

Desperately, he ran after the fishtailing Ford, finally throwing the glass at it and falling facefirst on the asphalt. We watched as he got up. He stood in the middle of the road looking around as if for a weapon. Blood dripped from him.

"I NEED A CAR!" screamed the Bull. "VERN!"

"Sorry, Bull, I'm nearly out of..."

This simple refusal seemed to send the Bull into a paroxysm of despair. He began bellowing, and joining his straightened arms in front of himself vaguely like the trunk of an elephant, he began to raise and lower this 'trunk' while he bellowed and ran around as if on a rampage.

Just then a small, inoffensive sedan towing a small, inoffensive caravan pulled into the parking bay near the store. Alan and Denise, the storekeepers, watched from the doorway of the shop. The caravan had an outline of Australia painted on the side in black and a red line indicated that they had come from Melbourne to Daytrap, nearly 300 miles, and still had the rest of Australia's coast to go. The sedan was nearly new and had a sign on the rear window that said "Running in. Please pass" . The driver was an old man. Through the tinted windows we could see the age spots on his hands. His wife was almost as old and terrifically fat.

The old couple were talking to each other. The Bull growled and ran towards the little car, still dripping blood. As he opened the driver's door the bewildered old man said, "Thank-you."

"KEYS!" roared Bull. "KEYS! I'M A POLICEMAN! THIS IS A MATTER OF LIFE AND DEATH! I'VE GOTTA KILL THE WOMAN I LOVE!"

The old man looked helplessly at the storekeepers. Denise covered her eyes with one hand and shook her head and said "It's only a car." Alan made the madness gesture with his finger and ear and then the 'what can I do?' gesture with his upturned palms. Bull took the keys from the old man's hand and got into the car.

"You can come if you want!" he said to the old woman who was still struggling to get out of her seatbelt. Then he drove.

But he only went twenty feet or so because the Fairlane gunned back into Daytrap and screeched to a bluesmoke halt. The driver slid over to the passenger's seat. The Bull abandoned the small sedan and the old woman in the middle of the road and ran to his car and got in and dropped a wheelie, pulling up next to the now shaking old man. He got out of the car pulling a fistful of notes from his jeans.

"You're beautiful man! Staunch, brother. You helped me when I was down! When no one else gave a stuff! Here! This is yours! I wish I had more to give ya! Come out and stay at the farm! Rage! Yaaaa!"

He shoved the money into the old man's breastpocket and kissed him passionately on the lips and then jumped in his car and roared off.

The old man blinked and simply said, "Thanks" and continued to shake violently. Denise and Alan took the old couple into their tea room for a cup of tea.

As he watched the Bull disappear up the road, Uncle Vern muttered in derision,

"Ferals! I know this is a free country and all that but we don't need that sort of thing. That Bull and his crew Reg, they are bad news. They have got no morals whatsoever. We'd be better off without 'em."

In my experience people who said they did not need this or that had little choice whether they got it or not. The country town was a small boat, in a way, like a coracle, full of primitive men painted blue. I could see why Uncle Vern did not simply grab the Bull and punch his lights out. Everyone had to live together. Besides, from what I had heard, the Bull, a man with little to lose, would simply have drunk a skinful and come round later with a shottie and blasted Uncle Vern and Auntie Mona's farmhouse, or worse.

Uncle Vern was still gazing after the Bull and his companion when another striking vehicle drove in the other side of Daytrap. It was an enormous, black Plymouth sedan, circa 1952. Cruising along at a leisurely, an imperial, pace, the vehicle had an innate majesty that rendered its few dents, scratches and rust spots almost unnoticeable.

In the backseat there was a kid a bit younger than me, maybe twelve or fourteen. He was dressed in a grey suit, and he stared intently from the back window at me. At the same time as I was curious about him - there were no other kids my age in the district - I was cautioned by the fixity of his stare. In the front passenger seat sat a middle-aged, middle-class woman. As they passed I heard the plangent strains of Donna Summer's famous disco hit, 'I Will Survive', and through the faded tinting of the front windows I saw something I knew was impossible: Rasputin himself was driving. As the car approached Polo's Daytrap Bridge Autoport Cafe it slowed and turned in and I noticed that the personalized number plate read 'CHRIST'.

Then Uncle Vern saw the car.

"The Holy Father! That's the Holy Father, Reg!" he said in a tone of awe. "Would you like to meet him?"

"Well," I began.

The three from the big Plymouth trooped into Polo's shop. The woman was maybe forty-five or fifty. The Holy Father, in the daylight, appeared to be in his twenties. Lank hair framed his lightly-bearded, pock-marked face. He wore a cassock. The woman was heavily made-up and wore a smart floral dress, surgical stockings and court shoes. Polo greeted them at the door of the cafe, as he always greeted everybody, and the Holy Father appeared to bestow some sort of blessing on Polo and his establishment as he entered.

"Come on!" said Uncle Vern. "They're stopping at Polo's! Maybe you can book in to get baptized!"

"I've already been confirmed, Uncle Vern," I said.

"You can be Born Again!" declared Uncle Vern.

"Who are the others, Uncle Vern?" I asked, thinking that they might be parishioners from an outlying farm.

"Why, they are his wife and child, Reg," said Uncle Vern.

"But I thought priests weren't supposed to marry," I said.

"In the Holy Father's church many things are possible that are not allowable in the conventional churches, Reg."

At the door of the cafe Polo greeted us without his usual reference to Pakistanis.

"Hello, Vernon! Hello Reginald! Praise the Lord!" he said.

With his eyes and thumb he indicated the presence of the Holy Father. The Holy Father was praying over the table with his eyes and hands clenched tight. Next to him his wife opened one eye and frankly stared at us for a moment then closed it again. Uncle Vern approached their table.

I stayed by Polo for the time being. Frankly, I did not like the look of the holy family. I try not to be prejudiced towards people when I know nothing of them, that is I try not to judge people only by their appearance but when it is all you know of a person, to some extent you have to. Uncle Vern waited as patiently as he could. Patience was never one of his strongest qualities.

The Holy Father's wife was a pretty, faded woman and she smelled strongly of 'Charlie', a perfume at least twenty years too young for her. This odour would have dominated even the strong pizza aroma of Polo's cafe had it not been for the heavy, mouse nest scent of the Holy Father.

The Holy Father was still praying. Polo went to the cappuccino machine and pulled the handle. The machine groaned and thick, rich coffee dribbled from the twin nozzles. Uncle Vern could not wait.

"Holy Father..." he ventured. "Holy Father."

The Holy Father's eyes relaxed slightly, then opened slowly. Uncle Vern smiled at him hopefully, even lovingly. The Holy Father's face contorted into a sly look.

"Brother Vern," he said in a deep voice, "Praise the Lord! Brother Vern, it is thee. Art thou good, Brother Vern."

"Praise the Lord, Holy Father!" said Uncle Vern. "It's real good to see you again and your lovely wife and child. Ma'am," he added, nodding to the wife real friendly-like.

"And hast thou been good, Brother Vern?" said the Holy Father somewhat pointedly, but still with his disquieting smile.

"I have been as good as I could be, Holy Father, Praise the Lord," said Uncle Vern, glancing nervously at me, "but I have been meaning to contact you for a little while now as it is some time since I was at communion and...."

"Confession!" said the Holy Father.

"Well, er, ..." said Uncle Vern.

He was glancing at the wife.

"Brother Vern," said the Holy Father. "It is necessary to sin in order to seek forgiveness, not that I advocate going out of one's way to seek sin out ... the devil is busy as we all know and attends us on all sides. The Lord loves the black sheep perhaps even above the white sheep and I am here to serve thee. I suggest, Brother Vern, that ye go now unto thine home and prepare thyself in prayer before baring thy soul to the Lord through my humble intercession. I shall finish this small libation with my family - we get so little time together, you know, pressure of the work, Praise the Lord - and we shall shortly be at your beautiful farm to join with you in fellowship with the Lord. And remember, Vern, when you pray, it is sincerity that counts above all else. God bless thee!" said the Holy Father, "And thee!" he added, nodding to me.

"Bless you, Holy Father, thank-you!" said Uncle Vern. "Ma'am!" he added, and he turned smartly on the heel of his William's riding boots and left the cafe. I followed. We crossed the road briskly and got into his Tojo and raced back to the Breakaways.

"The Holy Father, Reg," said Uncle Vern reverently, "has been in the district nearly a year now and his flock is growing each day because, because of his magnetism. He is inspirational, Reg, and he can perform miracles. Last month, just last month he brought back the dead. Dick Katz's dog, Darren Millane, was all but dead from a tick. The paralysis had set in and the breathing was almost gone. The Holy Father said, 'Bring forth the Caninite unto me.' He took the poor little thing - it was heartbreaking, Reg, because that dog Darren was very popular in the district - he took it in his arms, he did not care that it was covered in sputum and foam, and he put its entire head into his mouth and kept it there for a full minute...and when he took it out and released it that dog just ran straight out the hall and home and hid under the bed where Dick found it. A miracle! He plays hymns on a didgeridoo, Reg, because he believes in the holiness of this country, not Israel or Palestine or whatever you want to call it. Everything on earth is holy in the eyes of the Church of In and Out, Reg. Nothing is not natural and holy, nothing! And while he plays the hymns on the didgeridoo his beautiful wife and child sing harmonies from heaven. They come once a month, Reg. In and out. And no one knows where they live. But when you need the Holy Father he appears, miraculously. Another miracle. You know how that young couple out at the old Hodson farm, the Turveys, they was all but heartbroken because try as they might they could not have a little baby. Their marriage was on the rocks and then the Holy Father came along - like a thief in the night - in and out - and he counselled that young couple, and he gave them herbs to use and unguents and incantations and a personal session of spiritual guidance and sure enough, Praise the Lord, she fell pregnant. He is a good influence, the Holy Father!"

The flyscreen door at the kitchen squeaked as we entered and Uncle Vern called somewhat cautiously,

"Mona...Mona?" but she was out.

"That's good!" said Uncle Vern. "Your Auntie Mona was brought up a strict Methodist, and she does not like the Holy Father. Some of those conservative religions do not like those that reach back to the origins of religion, that ask the hard questions, the ones that provide the unashamed answers...they are mere Sunday religions and they do not cater for the complete man, as the Holy Father's Church of In and Out does."

Uncle Vern retired to his bedroom. He emerged soon after dressed entirely in black and sporting a large gold neckchain with the circle and cross symbol resting on his thick bush of stick-on chest hair that he had gotten from Bernard's Magic Shop the last time he was in Melbourne.

"Wait here for the Holy Father, Reg. When he comes tell him that I have gone down to Sabrina's grave to pray. Send him down there." Then he took off.

Sabrina, the dog Uncle Vern owned before he married Auntie Mona, was buried out by the toolshed. I practised my whittling on the verandah as I waited for the Holy Father to come. At length the big Plymouth slunk around the serpentine curves of the Daytrap road, swung into the driveway and slunk up to where I was. The kid in the back was still staring at me. The Holy father's wife looked me up and down. The Holy Father himself leapt from the car with surprising agility and almost ran around to me, all the time looking over his shoulders and round about. I noticed that he wore odd socks with his leather sandals.

His arm seemed to elongate as it reached out for me and wrapped itself around my shoulder.

"You must be Reginald," he said, very unctiously. "Your dear Uncle has told me so much about you, Reginald. You are a very special boy!" he said, looking over his shoulder. "Where is your Uncle?"

"Uncle Vern has gone to pray behind the toolshed," I said.

The Holy Father still had his arm around me. His wife was looking at me with some consternation, I thought. The boy in the back seat was now smiling idiotically.

"Do you know what the name Reginald means, Reginald?" asked the Holy Father.

"No," I said

"Queenly. It means queenly. Like a queen. Beloved of queens. It's from the Latin, Regina, you can see it on the back of coins. Isn't that nice!" said the Holy Father.

"I'll show you where Uncle Vern is," I said, running ahead.

When we neared the toolshed I called to Uncle Vern.

"Uncle Vern!" I called.

He did not answer. When we came upon him, he was lost in prayer.

"Oh, Lord! Lord! Lord, have mercy upon a hopeless sinner. I know Mona has not been a well woman..."

The Holy Father attracted his attention with a small neck massage.

"Oh, oh, Holy Father, it is thee!" said Uncle Vern. "Pardon me, Lord, I have visitors."

"The Lord abide with thee, Brother Vern!" said the Holy Father. "Arise, Brother Vern, for the Lord has selected thee for a special task this day. A celebratory office has fallen unto thee, Brother Vern. After thou hadst left Brother Polo's worthy establishment Brother Bull and Sister Blue were sent unto me by the Lord in his wisdom and they besought me to join them, that is, unite them, in Holy Wedlock. We are needful of a witness, Brother Vern, and you were the first sinner we thought of. Can you come out to their farm at once, Brother Vern? Bring young Reginald, too, yea, verily, by all means, suffer the little children to come. But quickly, Brother Vern, it is a matter of urgency! They may change their minds at any minute."

Uncle Vern looked disappointed.

"Gee, Holy Father, I mean, I'm hardly dressed..."

"Nonsense, Brother Vern, thine cerements beeth ideal."

"But Holy Father, what about my confession?"

"Thou hast a prior duty unto thine neighbor, Brother Vern. I may always attend to thine confession. Come, we must hasten. Follow with thine Tojo!"

With that the Holy Father turned and swept away in his robes. We got into the car and flew down the drive, passing the Plymouth. Uncle Vern was speeding but very casually and he shot the wife a cool two-fingered salute from the brim of his hat.

"Normally, Reg, I would not bother with the Bull, but the Holy Father has asked so...pass me the California Poppy, son."

I got his hair oil out of the glove box. Uncle Vern drove with his knees as he squirted some of the oil onto his palm and then rubbed it through his hair. He took his comb from his breast pocket and slicked back his hair just like Elvis.

We left the highway and sped along a broad and firm though slightly corrugated timber track.

"I think it's the last one on the left before Big Flat Creek Track," said Uncle Vern.

We passed a number of wrecks along the way.

"There's his old Studebaker!" said Uncle Vern.

"There's his old De Soto!"

"There's his old Mustang!"

Thus we kept on the right track. At length the road lead us down into a dank, rainforest gully and we followed a stream for a couple of kilometres until we came to a ramshackle wooden gate hanging by one hinge and opening onto a broad meadow of river flat. At the high edge of the meadow were two slab huts, a small orchard and an unkempt kitchen garden. Various livestock - cows, goats, pigs - and several vehicles were scattered about the flat. Uncle Vern parked some distance from the huts facing the Tojo towards the gate.

"A precaution," he said. "You never know with the Bull. He changes faster than the weather. Jesus! I haven't brought a wedding present!"

He closed the door. "Thank Gawd for that!" he said as he noticed his two supplementary slabs of beer in the tray.

"Two slabs! Ideal! Come on, Reg, bring them slabs! We might as well get this over with!"

The Plymouth pulled up alongside us and Uncle Vern tipped his hat and said "Ma'am!" to the Holy Father's wife.

The Bull lurched from a hut swinging a bottle of champagne and zipping the jeans which were his only garment.

"Brothers!" he cried when he saw us. "And sister! Sorry, man, I nearly forgot your old lady!" he added, addressing the Holy Father. "Come on out here ya mole whether yer decent or not! We got guests! Blue!" he roared.

"Happy wedding, Bull!" said Uncle Vern. "I hope yez have a good marriage. We brung a little present... it's not much..."

Uncle Vern indicated me. I proffered the slabs.

"Yeah, oh beautiful man!" said the Bull, "Ya shouldn't have, but since ya did put 'em in the freezer on the verandah, man, they'll be safe in there, for a few minutes."

When I got to the freezer I found that it had vertical doors which I could not open because the body of a man was in front of them. I looked back at the Bull.

"Oh, that's Fleegle, man. Just kick him out of the way. He won't mind. He won't even notice it."

I tried to move him gently with my foot.

"No, no man, ya gotta kick him," said the Bull patiently. "Here, I'll show ya."

And he came over and started kicking his friend with great force, mainly in the head, until his bulky form gradually shifted away from the freezer.

"See!" said the Bull.

The men stood round laughing at this, even the Holy Father.

"Poor brother Fleegle," said the Holy Father, drinking liberally from the champagne.

Bull offered a flask of Jim Beam to the preacher's wife but she politely demurred.

Music came from within the huts. Roy Orbison's 'The Penny Arcade'. Then the Bull's bride emerged from the hut in a cheesecloth shift and smoking a large, homemade cigarette. The breeze that was making its leisurely way down the valley blew her garment against her and revealed a surprisingly substantial tummy, and other things not so surprising. I noticed Uncle Vern becoming somewhat thyroid.

"Sister Blue," said the Holy Man, "How lovely to see thee on this auspicious day of thine betrothal!" He kissed her lightly on the cheek. Uncle Vern lined up behind him and kissed her noisily on the neck. She maintained an air of indifference.

"Thanks, man," she said.

"Now, Brother Bull," said the Holy Man, as the Bull was opening another bottle of champagne, "What sort of wedding do you want, Praise the Lord."

The Bull took a swig of champagne and said, "I want a graceful wedding!"

"Yeah. Far out!" said Blue.

"My woman...my lady...and I want a simple wedding. We want a rite that suits us. I want something to celebrate in the eyes of God the incredible love that this woman here has for me and I have for her."

So saying he grabbed one of Blue's breasts with one hand and slammed his own fist and forearm against his chest.

"Beautiful," said Uncle Vern, looking at Blue. " Isn't that beautiful, Reg," .

"Ok," said the Holy Father, " I think we can fix that. Now where do you want to do it?"

"Anywhere, man, anywhere!" leered the Bull and he and Uncle Vern laughed heartily.

"Under the Lillipilli tree," said Blue.

"Let's do it!" said the Holy Father and we all trooped towards the big lillipilli behind the huts.

The Bull was drinking from the flask of Jim Beam and he handed it about generously.

"Getitinya, Vern, bro!" he urged.

My Uncle needed little encouragement. He had a long, soothing draught. Then he carefully wiped the mouth with his sleeve and offered the bottle to the Holy Father's wife but she declined somewhat nervously,

"No, thank-you very much, I do not drink spirits. In fact I drink nothing in the daytime," she said.

"Oh, pardon me," said Uncle Vern with genuine sincerity as he had another sip.

The Holy Father stood by the tree trunk and we gathered before him. Uncle Vern, who was sort of like the best man stood by the Bull. The Holy Father's wife stood by Blue. Their son was nowhere to be seen. The Holy Father noticed this and said,

"Where is Edric?"

"He's in the car," said his wife, "he is not feeling very well."

"Oh," said the Holy Father. "Well. Friends.." he began, sonorously.

"Wait!" cried the Bull. "Wait, it's not right! . It's gotta be natural!" declared the Bull. "Get yer gear off! All of it! Off! Now!"

"But.." said Uncle Vern.

"But..." said the Holy Man's wife.

"Ooo-kay." said the Holy Father, simply. "The old Albigensian way."

The Holy Father's wife whispered to him. The Holy Father whispered to the Bull who was already naked. I was amazed at how red he was. There was hardly any space at all between his freckles. The Bull said, "Okay." The Holy Father whispered to his wife and the lady began to undress. Blue was already in the buff as they say. Uncle Vern looked as if he had contracted lockjaw. Gathering his wits he went to the Bull and whispered urgently to him. The Bull burst out laughing and shouted loudly,

"Skidmarks! Vern's got skidmarks! Off with 'em Vern!" he said and he began helping Uncle Vern to achieve an unspoiled state. I could see how things were going so I voluntarily took off my clothes. It wasn't much worse than the showers at school and I knew it could not last forever. As I was undressing I noticed the Holy Father looking intently at me. I wasn't sure where I should stand. I was the only person who did not have something to do.

"Come, my son," Holy Father said. "Stand hard by me here and hold this." He gave me a thick stick of sandalwood and lit it.

We were all naked except for the Holy Father's wife who retained her foundation garments. Uncle Vern, shamed as he was, still managed to smile courteously at the two women as the ceremony began again.

"Friends, welcome!" said the Holy Father. "In the eyes of God the joining of man and woman is the pinnacle of creation. Thus to marry a man and a woman in the eyes of the Lord is the highest office in the church. Hundreds of years ago, when services in the old church were hardly solemn at all, the marriage ceremony was the gravest of all celebrations, and retained strong ties with pagan practice."

"Right on!" said the Bull.

As the Holy Father spoke I watched the four people before me. The Holy Father's wife was as rigid as whalebone with embarrassment. Uncle Vern was suffering an attack of priapism. Sister Blue, was casual, even indifferent. The Bull was listening intently to what the Holy Man had to say until suddenly he remembered something and hissed to Uncle Vern,

"Have you got a ring?"

"Jeez, no!" Uncle Vern hissed back.

But Uncle Vern was a resourceful country man, a master of improvisation. He cast his eyes about and found what he needed: the ring pull from a beer can. He stooped quickly, wrapped the tongue of it around the ring part and showed it to the Bull. The Bull looked impressed and grateful. The Holy Father did not allow them to interrupt him.

"I would have ye bear this in mind and be ye mindful also of this: that when a man and a woman are bound together in matrimony, in the eyes of the Lord God Our Father it is as if these two die, and they are replaced by new life. This is the myth of the Phoenix: life from fire and death! Marriage, and implicit in marriage, procreation, are the crux of life in all the universe, brothers and sisters and I want that ye should think hard upon the consequences of marriage under heaven and above hell as these two beautiful creatures come forth to be wed. Come forth, Brother Bull. Come forth, Sister Blue."

The Bull, winking at Uncle Vern, led his bride by one of her nose rings.

"Ow! Stoppit Bull, that hurts," she said.

"Join hands, please," said the Holy Father.

They did so.

"It must pleaseth the Lord something powerful to see here before him two young people who have tested their love in the furnace of life and found it to be true and who now wish to solemnize their miraculous discovery of each other! Amen! Brother Bull, before you renounce your life as an individual, and submerge it in the life of your Sister, Blue, is there anything you wish to say?"

"Yeah!" said the Bull. Then he seemed at a loss for words. "What, er, what I reckon, is that what is mine is hers. My friends are her friends. My farm is her farm. My grog is her grog. My enemies are her enemies. My debts are her debts. Her grog is my grog. We are gonna be solid man, solid! Yeah! Rage!"

"Sister Blue, is there any statement you wish to make before we tie this indissoluble knot?"

"Statement? What? Nah, not really."

"The ring," said the Holy Father.

Uncle Vern stepped forward holding one hand over his private parts as he handed the ring to the Bull. The Holy Father seemed slightly amused and said,

"We are all naked before God, Brother Vern. It is customary for the best man and the maid of honour to stand closer together during the penultimate part of the rite!" he added motioning with his hand that my Uncle and the Holy Father's wife stand closer together.

I felt sorry for my Uncle knowing how ashamed he was of his polio stricken legs, and knowing how he hated having to struggle with his constant attacks of priapism. Not that he was displeased at close proximity with the woman, yet he was hardly in control of the circumstances. I myself felt somewhat uncomfortable near the Holy Father.

"Place the finger on the bride's ring!" commanded the Holy Father

The Bull did so. The Holy Father, noticing the humble ring said.

"It is the thought which doth count. Baby Jesus was born unto a manger. The ringpull is a symbol just as much as the band of gold. Perhaps even more spiritual in view of its other associations. Be not disappointed or ashamed, Sister Blue, Brother Bull has honoured thee today. Do you Brother Bull take thy Sister Blue as thine wife."

"Oh, yeah." said the Bull.

"And do thee, Sister Blue, take this man, thy Brother Bull, as thine husband?"

"I s'pose so." she said.

"Then!" said the Holy Father, "ye are husband and wife, may death alone part ye. Thou mayst now kisseth the bride, Brother Bull."

"I'll do better than that!" declared the Bull. He pushed her against the tree and began to consummate the marriage.

The Holy Father seemed amused. Uncle Vern was growing excited by the spectacle. The Holy Father's wife was transfixed. Uncle Vern was becoming concerned for her welfare when I thought I should attend to something at the car. I grabbed my clothes and ran. The Holy Father at once began to chase me. He called after me ,

"Reg! Reggie! Come back, Reg. It is only natural and the will of God! Come back!"

I ran right around the property with the Holy Father chasing after me, seeking to comfort me. When I emerged into the clearing again, by the Lillipilli tree, the Bull and his new wife were watching Uncle Vern struggling on the ground with the Holy Father's wife. I felt there was safety in numbers and watched also.

"Uncle Vern! Uncle Vern!" I called but he did not hear. The Holy Father when he arrived also watched.

Stopping for a breather, Uncle Vern saw us all watching him and turned bright red.

"Holy Father!" he exclaimed, "Help me, Holy Father!"

"You seem to be doing quite well, Brother Vern." said the Holy Father.

"Oh Holy Father, I do not know what came over me. I must have been possessed by some demon!" said Uncle Vern

"Do not worry thyself, Brother Vern," said the Holy Father.

The Bull saved the situation from any possible awkwardness by producing bottles of Jim Beam and champagne and the company toasted the wedding. Uncle Vern, being in more familiar territory, proposed the toast: ' To the Bride and Groom and a happy life'. Then, jokingly, the way people joke at weddings, he asked the Bull what the hell he would want to get married for, at his age, when he could be expected to know better.

The Bull changed suddenly and became dreadfully angry.

"All my life," shouted the Bull, "I have been surrounded by ugliness and stupidity and misfortune.

I starved as a child and was sexually molested constantly, my little brother died, I was orphaned at twelve and arrested fifty-three times before I was seventeen and I have been branded as bad ever since. I have been in sixteen fatal car crashes and I have tried to kill myself four times and like everything else I have ever tried I failed every time. I have lived in institutions for twenty of the last twenty-five years! I have had two hundred different diseases, Vernon!" he yelled into my Uncle's face, "And now at last when I have met this beautiful woman, my soulmate, the first thing that has ever gone right in my whole entire life I want to grab it with both hands and squeeze every last drop of joy from it because it is the first and last chance I will ever have in this miserable world to find happiness. And do you know what we are gonna do?" At this he tenderly grasped his new wife's tummy. "We are gonna do the most beautiful thing you can do man: we are gonna make a baby! We have made a baby! It is gonna be the most beautiful baby there ever was and we are gonna give this baby everything - EVERYTHING! - do you hear me? - Everything that a baby can have and everything in life that we never had, all the chances we never had, all the love we never had. Do you understand what I am saying Vern, or have you been dead for so long that you can't understand these simple dreams any more? We are gonna remake the world Vern, and that is the biggest and best thing that a man can aspire to do and we are

          An Uncle Vern Story: Pedestrians Watch Your Step!

gonna do it the right way. That is why we invited the Holy Father and youse here today, so that we could, with your help, reach nearer to God and take a chance on his blessing for our rocky voyage over life's ocean of tears!"

He clenched his teeth and fists and growled fiercely and slammed his right forearm across his chest. He punched himself hard on the nose.

"Don't you know what it is all about, Vern? It is all about hope, Vern! Hope! Hope, you drunken bastard. Now get off my place if you can't understand that. I'M WARNING YOU VERN, YOU DON'T KNOW WHAT A WILDMAN IS!"

These things said, growling and gnashing his teeth, the Bull ran to his verandah and grabbed a shotgun that was sitting there. He pointed it at Uncle Vern and pulled both triggers. Nothing happened.

"Where's the shells, woman?" he demanded of Sister Blue. "It's your job to look after the ammo!" . He began to rummage around the rubbish on the verandah for his shells. We needed no further encouragement to take our leave.

"Thanks for having us," I said as we ran by. "Nice to meet you!"

The Holy Father and his wife ran with us.

"I'll collect my fee next week, Bull," he called.

"Father," said Uncle Vern as we sped towards the vehicles clutching our clothes, " I will be needing a confession and perhaps an exorcism next week."

"Certainly, Brother Vern, certainly," agreed the unconventional cleric. "Like a thief in the night, I shall be there."

Shots passed harmlessly overhead as we cleared the Bull's gateway. Uncle Vern swore that he would never be coming there again and all the way home he expatiated on the evil that was marriage.

CUT AND COME AGAIN

a slice of life

An Uncle Vern story: Unfit For Human Consumption

Uncle Vern had agreed to help Lennie Johnson muster some half-wild cattle from the hills around Nungatta and he had taken me along for the ride. Hitherto I had only ridden Auntie Mona's placid brood mare, Virginia - or Ginny, as we called her for short - around and around the corral, but here I was on one of Lennie's stallions riding along a wild spur, perhaps never traversed by whitemen before on the lower slopes of the Great Divide. The scene before us was breathtaking. Far below the silver river tinkled silently down to the sea. Uncle Vern stretched forth his hand indicating the vista like an Indian Chief, and said,

"Look at that! Louis Buvelot might have painted that!"

Those who had only a passing acquaintance with Uncle Vern would probably be surprised to find that he was an art lover. A man who was always up at the crack of rosy-fingered dawn, who worked so hard it was pathetic to see at times, to the outside world

Uncle Vern appeared an ordinary, middle-aged, country lout, so aptly described by the poet:

"..a horny-handed son of toil,

of wire and strain, of broken fingernail and soil,

in his arse a lonely ache, and on his back a boil."

Yet, as a youth, the flame of a passion for art had been kindled when he found a book of artists' studies at the Daytrap tip. Though living in the country limited his opportunities for extending his knowledge of art, over the years he had amassed a library of pictures and the walls of the farmhouse were bedecked with paintings. In the loungeroom there was a crepuscular Hans Heysen by the window, over the fireplace Landseer's 'Monarch of the Glen', and behind the door a cerise and vermilion 'Junk at Sunset in Macau' by Long Dong; in the kitchen Van Gogh's 'Potato Eaters', and Hals' 'Laughing Cavalier'; in the hall there was a bold concession to modernism: Nolan's Ned Kelly paintings; only one painting hung in the toilet, The Girl From Ipanema in the fork of a tree above a green lagoon with raven hair and that alluring smile painted by anonymous. These were all prints, of course. The highlight of the collection was in the bedroom: a large, lubricious, original, Norman Lindsay, hanging on the wall at the foot of the bed.

Apart from the Lindsay, the collection of pictures was eclectic and predictable. But Uncle Vern's particular interest in art was more evident in his library which he kept in a locked cabinet. He never actually showed me these treasures of his, though sometimes I would come upon him poring almost ecstatically over a book of Rubens or Degas, Michaelangelo, Gaughin, Felicien de Rops, Lindsay, Beardsley, Modigliani, Goya, Bosch and even Lucas Cranach the Elder. He had clearly thought deeply upon them over many years of long, lonely farmhouse nights. He would occasionally muse aloud upon the artists that interested him so much. For instance he maintained that Degas was 'spoiled by being a lace-fiend'. Bosch had 'a dirty mind but went too far'. Gaughin was 'a poxy bastard'. Michaelangelo 'never saw a naked woman in his life'. Cranach was evidence of how much women had improved over the years due to sound breeding practices. His greatest admiration was reserved for Modigliani who, he said, had so severely damaged his feet, hands and mouth in a caravan fire that he had been forced to paint with a brush strapped to his male organ. That was why he only ever painted nudes: it was the only way he could hold a brush straight.

"It sure is a great spot, Uncle Vern!" I said.

"Yes, Reg, it's not bad at all. But there's no nude! Can you see a nude, Reg?"

I looked around, wondering what he meant and said,

"No, Uncle Vern."

"Neither can I son. No landscape is complete without a nude. Remember that. No interior is complete without a nude. Above all, no nude is complete without another nude to set it off."

"Gee, Uncle Vern, how did you get to learn so much about art?"

"I don't know so much about art son," said Uncle Vern, with his usual air of false modesty. "I used to be interested in art once, but as I grew older I became more engaged with the real thing: Life Itself. I was once young and idealistic, Reg. I really believed in ideals. And I thought artists were the people that pursued those ideals, no matter what. Degas and the perfect ballerina; John and the perfect boy; Constable and the perfect barnyard animals, Reg. But like all idealism it was pummelled out of me by actual experience of real life. There was an artist who lived in this district some years ago now, boy, and I learnt as much about art as I will ever want to know from him."

"Really, Uncle Vern! Who was he?"

"His name was Norman Lindsay," said Uncle Vern matter-of-factly.

"You knew Norman Lindsay, Uncle Vern?" I asked, deeply impressed.

"Yeah, I knew him," said Uncle Vern, as if he wished he hadn't. "Do you want to know about him, son?"

"Sure, Uncle Vern, whatever you think is suitable."

Our mounts were picking their way along the ridge without our doing much. Uncle Vern rolled a smoke with one hand, then dropped it accidentally and rolled another with two hands and then he said at length,

"I knew Lindsay. His family had a big house up on the Brown Mountain, and when we were riding stock through that way I used to call in on him at times. His family goes back a ways in this district like mine does. He gave my mother that picture in the bedroom which she left to me. When I was a boy he even showed me a bit about painting. Despite the stories of loose living we used to hear from time to time, I thought he was all right - until I found out the truth about the Magic Pudding. Do you know what the Magic Pudding was, son?"

"I have read the book, Uncle Vern. It was a terrific book, too."

"I ask it again," said Uncle Vern, as if to a third party. "Do you know what the Magic Pudding was?"

"A book."

"No."

"A story?"

"Nope."

"A pudding?"

"A pudding? A pudding, you say? What sort of a pudding, Reg?"

"Well, any sort," I said, somewhat impatiently.

"I'll give you a clue son. Skinny legs."

"A chicken pie?"

"Another clue. A sour expression."

"Lemon Chiffon pie?"

"It always tried to run away."

"Rabbit?"

"Big lips."

"Fish pie?"

"Cut and come again! What could it mean?"

"I don't know, Uncle Vern!"

"What gets bigger the more you take away?"

"A hole," I said.

"Correct at last! Now, black face. Last clue, black face."

I looked at him blankly.

"Damn it all Reg, the Magic Pudding was a woman, an Aboriginal woman, boy! A lubra! A gin! Now that you know, is it, or is it not, as obvious as all hell?"

"It's obvious, Uncle Vern, real obvious! I am amazed they are allowed to sell it in shops."

"Not only that, Reg but I can tell you her name because Norman Lindsay never made up a story in his entire life. He heard about that woman and the bushmen from his father!"

"Really, Uncle Vern?"

"Yep, really! I know because the original Bill Barnacle was your Great-great-grandad Rodney. Bunyip Bluegum was based on old Cyril and Sam Sawnoff was Young Roy, or, more to the point, I should say, they were not them. Those characters were nothing but caricatures, Reg, and it is a pity because behind the Magic Pudding lay a true and tragic story, a story that reverberates even today in this callous age. Would you like to hear about it, Reg?"

"I sure would, Uncle Vern!" I said.

Her real name was Hopping Kitty, that's not counting her tribal name which nobody knew anyway. They called her Hopping Kitty because she walked with a limp on account of her being shot in the foot when she was just a little girl. And your Great-great-grandfather Rodney bought her from a Chinaman. In the book they say he is a cook but you just have to take one look at him and you can see straightaway that he is a Chinaman. It's obvious once you know, Reg. They had observed him when he came through the district. The dogs started to disappear and they knew right away what was getting on. But they were more concerned about the plight of the poor young native girl he kept and fearfully mistreated.

They went up to this Chinaman straightout, no mucking about, and they offered him ten pounds for the lubra. He readily agreed. Roy suggested giving him another five pounds to leave the district, but Grandad Rodney had a better idea. He said to the greedy Chinaman,

"Foo Loo, you too are an Australian, and you'll do me for a rough mate any day. I think you have done us a square deal with this here lubra and I want to help you, too, Foo Loo."

"Velly goo!" said Foo Loo.

"I know a place where there are hundreds of nice, fat stray dogs running around free just for the grabbin'."

"Leally?" said Foo Loo. "Where day are, Lodney?"

"Not so far from here, Foo Loo, at Lambing Flat."

"Oh, Lodney, Kyow! Kyow velly much. Rambing Frat. Kyow velly much!"

And with that he was gone. That stuff in the book about them killing that Chinaman by pushing him off the iceberg was all bull! They never harmed a hair on his head! It was a fair and square deal all round. The Chinaman was pleased with his ten quid. Hopping Kitty was happy to be out of the clutches of the wicked oriental and the men were happy to have been able to do her a good turn.

"Have you ever looked for a long time at the pictures of the Magic Pudding, Reg?"

"What do you mean, Uncle Vern."

"I mean have you ever applied what they call in the art business, The Gaze, to her?"

"What do you mean, Uncle Vern?"

"What does she look like?"

"Oh, er, plain, Uncle Vern, very plain."

"Plain? Ugly! Real ugly, I'd say! And bad tempered too, if you can believe what you read. According to that Norman Lindsay she was real grouchy and was always trying to run away from Rodney and Roy and Cyril. But it wasn't true.

"That Norman Lindsay had an axe to grind, Reg. For his very own father was a pudding thief. One of the most notorious pudding thieves in the district in his day. You have a look at them pudding thieves in the book and tell me that that possum is not pure Lindsay. He was always trying to lure Hopping Kitty away to live at the big house on the hill, but she wouldn't go. No. Because the three bushmen treated her well. They rewrite history, Reg, all the time. Just turn your back on 'em for a moment and they'll rewrite it every time.

"At first she was shy, terrible shy, but she began to open up as she grew used to the men and their ways. She gradually became sociable. They taught her about hard liquor. She had a sense of humour and laughed at their jokes. She got used to their ways and they got used to her ways.

"You know how it says in the book that the Pudding liked to be eaten regularly? Well, that was true.

"Now them pictures of the Pudding in the book are what you might call first glance pictures. At first glance Hopping Kitty looked very, very plain to the men. And her ways seemed very rude, even to them. Nevertheless they realized that she had needs, womanly needs, including, among other things, being eaten regularly, and they all shared equally the responsibility of attending to these needs. Because she was their mate and she was doing her bit around the place...it was the least they could do, Reg. After all she did washing and the cooking and kept the camp clean and she rode out with them as good as any man could. She worked hard tending their mangel-wurzels. She might have been skinny, but she was strong and a good worker.

"In return for their helping her improve her English Hopping Kitty taught them about the bush foods and secret sources of water and medicines for their many ailments. She was a good prospector too.

"After a time Hopping Kitty turned out to be not so ugly at all. Though the word 'comb' meant nothing to her whatsoever there was an appealing wildness and a freedom about her unkempt wavy brown locks tinged blond by the outdoors life. Her teeth she kept white by chewing charcoal and when she smiled it was like the moonrise. Her cheeks shone when she laughed and she laughed all day long. (In that book she only scowled because she only ever scowled when she saw a Lindsay, Reg, and that's the truth.)

"Propinquity is a marvellous thing, Reg, one of the great unsung wonders of human intercourse. "

"What's propinquity, Uncle Vern? "

"Propinquity, son, is closeness, nearness, proximity, especially in the personal sense involving people, like the three bushmen were close, like Chang and Eng and like, say, you and me, Reg. If people spend time close together they grow closer and closer. Propinquity can even make a plain woman comely, Reg, and that is a wonderful thing, is it not? "

"Oh, yes, Uncle Vern , "I said.

Uncle Vern fell silent for a time as we negotiated a steep gully. Coming to the bottom, a narrow creek, we stopped to water our mounts.

"Yes, Reg. Propinquity worked its magic between Hopping Kitty and the men. Pretty soon the camp just about revolved around Hopping Kitty. She learnt to sew - Great-Grandad Rodney taught her that - and she mended their clothes. She learnt to read and write and kept accounts and wrote letters for them. Best of all, every night around the campfire, she used to sing to the men and tell them stories from the vast trove of native lore handed down to her by her tribe that had been destroyed by history.

"It maybe that there was magic in those songs, Reg. Black magic. They say the Aboriginal woman can sing to the man she wants and after that he has no chance: he is hers. Maybe it was magic that affected them, who knows and who cares? When you're on a good thing stick to it!

"Old Cyril, and young Roy, they always maintained that that was the best camp they ever had. Everyone in the district was jealous because their camp was so well run. The mangel-wurzels promised to yield them a small fortune that autumn. Hopping Kitty was happy, the men were happy. It was a happy camp, Reg, perhaps the happiest camp there ever was in this country! But it could not last, Reg, nothing lasts forever, good or bad.

"One morning young Roy was left alone at the camp because he had a bad tummy ache. The others were out tending the mangel-wurzels. He was having a quiet cup of tea when Annie, their kelpie cross slut - that was what they called bitches in those days, Reg - started making an awful fuss.

"Roy was surprised to see a group of myall blacks come in from the scrub. They were Adam naked and armed with spears and boomerangs. Roy knew if he was to make any sudden move like for the Martini-Henry he had inside the hut he would be a dead man. The blackfellers approached him cautiously and seemed friendly enough. They looked carefully about at the tracks.

"Roy offered them a cup of tea. They knew about tea and sat and drank some with him from the billy can. By means of signs and the few words of English they had they managed to converse.

"You gottem woman, "they said.

"Yeah. So what, "said Roy, expecting the worst.

"OK. "they said.

"They did not mind. For they believed that after a native woman had been with white men then she was spoiled for the tribal life. Once she got a taste for dresses and socks, hard liquor, cooking with pots, foreplay, winning domestic fights and other features of our way of life, that was it, she could not go back to the old, hard ways.

"While the black men did not mind that Roy and his mates had Hopping Kitty, they did think that they ought to have something on account, as it were. Roy, being democratic, thought that this was fair enough. He gave them a knife and a few quids of Sunlight chewing tobacco, a couple of old blankets and a twenty-pound bag of rice, lovely, shiny rice which they were much taken with. They wanted some bullets, too, not knowing what they were for. Roy told them that you needed a gun to fire them, but he couldn't make them understand, so he let them have them anyway. Then they melted into the scrub as if they'd never been.

"That night at the camp the others agreed that young Roy had done the right thing, though Cyril thought he had been a bit over-generous with the tobacco.

                   An Uncle Vern story: Unfit For Human Consumption

"The next morning at dawn the men were awakened by angry shouting from the edge of their camp. Emerging from their hut in nothing but their longjohns they were confronted by an angry mob of blacks who had treacherously armed themselves with a firearm and appeared intent on massacring the white men.

"' Is this how you filthy blacks treat the kindness of the whiteman? ' shouted Great-Grandad Rodney, a man who never backed down from nothing.

"All they could do was to gibber at him in their lingo. They was all yelling, kicking up a fearful fuss. Then Kitty came out of the hut and everything was quiet. She shouted to the myalls, asking them what the matter was.

"They had a long talk with her, an angry talk.

"Kitty explained to the men that they were accusing young Roy of poisoning them. The rice was poisoned, they said. Several of their people had died after eating it. Their bellies had swelled up and they just died. Then Roy realized what had happened.

"' Gee, ya know, I think I forgot to tell them how to cook it. ' he said.

"It was all a misunderstanding, Reg, that's all it was.

"Hopping Kitty tried to explain this but the Aborigines were not to be molified. They got angrier and angrier. They were working themselves up into a frenzy. The spears and boomerangs began to fly. As the natives advanced on the camp the air was full of shouting and confusion.

"Gread-grandad Rodney tried to take Hopping Kitty by the hand and she dived in front of him as the black with the gun fired and she took the bullet. They fell to the ground together. The blacks were momentarily stunned by this display of self-sacrifice. Old Cyril managed to get to the Martini-Henry and he began firing. The blacks took flight, but not before Cyril had winged a couple. But that was no help to Hopping Kitty. She lay in Grandad Rodney's arms, dying. The last thing she said was in her own language, so we'll never know what it was, son. The three men were stricken with remorse about what had occurred."

"What a day of tragic waste, Uncle Vern," I said.

"Yes, Reg," said Uncle Vern, fighting back real tears. "No more pudding after that! No more pudding for anyone, black, white or brindle."

Uncle Vern paused, and then added bitterly,

"That was the end of that camp. The men grew listless and took to the drink. The mangel-wurzels rotted in the fields and they wandered away from that part of the country never to return."

We kept riding along the creek in silence for a long time. It was reassuring, and yet sad too, to know that we were not going to be attacked by a party of Aborigines as we made our peaceful way through the country. At length we saw a frail pillar of smoke rising above the trees ahead of us. We were nearly back at Lennie's stock camp. There'd be a well stewed pot of tea on the stove waiting for us, undoubtedly, and some damper and salt beef to fill our stomach's. And Lennie's cheerful company to keep the ghost of Hopping Kitty at bay.

"Nearly home, Reg," said Uncle Vern. "Did you like the story of Hopping Kitty, or the Magic Pudding, Reg."

"It was real interesting, Uncle Vern. But I still don't really see what Norman Lindsay did that was so bad."

"What! Good heavens Reg! What are you, a moral leper? That man shamelessly depicted good, honest bushmen as animals! The men who carved a nation out of this godforsaken place! He mocked their beautiful relationship with Hopping Kitty out of sheer jealousy because his own father was nothing but a pudding thief and never a pudding owner. That man took something that was natural and good and sacred, Reg, sacred, and beautiful and dammit all Reg, heartbreakingly tragic in the end, heartbreakingly tragic as she died at the fumbling hands of the ignorant remnants of her people, Reg, that man Lindsay, he could paint all right, he was a genius, a twisted genius, but he should never have done what he did!"

"What did he do, Uncle Vern?" I asked, anxiously.

"He made a joke of it! The bastard made a joke of the whole thing. I can never forgive him for that."

Lennie was waiting for us when we got to his log cabin. His gimlet eyes watched as we dismounted and he said around his cigarette,

"Find anythin' Vern?"

"Nah," said Uncle Vern, "nah, there's nothin' whatsoever in rat gully, not even tracks."

"That's too bad," said Lennie.

"Yeah, nothin'!" said Uncle Vern, "so I told Reg about Hopping Kitty."

"Hoppin' Kitty, eh?" said Lennie. "Ya know the Yowies got her, son. Bad business. Come in an' I'll tell ya all about it."

Uncle Vern quietly caught my eye and winked to let me know that Lennie's story was likely to be embroidered at the least.

THE PRICKLY PEAR

a fairy tale

An Uncle Vern Story: Hardhats Must Be Worn On Site

Uncle Vern's footsteps came down the hall and ever closer to my door, just like Lon Chaney Jr. in 'The Return of the Mummy'. Stomp! Scrape! Stomp! Scrape! Stomp! Scrape! There was nothing I could do. I pulled my dressing gown tightly about me and wrapped the cord four times around and tied a double bow.

Uncle Vern was in his work clothes. Perhaps he wouldn't stay. There was hope.

"Hello, Uncle Vern!" I said as brightly as one could expect a person supposedly suffering from pneumonia to say anything. "Are you gonna put the snig track into Rat Gully today?"

"Too windy!" he said. "And too wet. That damn forestry fool won't let us in. I do not know what this world is coming to when bushmen are not allowed into the bush anymore on the sayso of some ill-bred university-educated young ignoramus!"

"Oh," I said. "That's no good, Uncle Vern!" I knew how much he enjoyed putting in snig tracks and snigging out logs.

"Aaaahhh, never mind, Reg. I suppose it gives me a chance to cheer you up a bit in your sick bed. How's the breathing?"

"It's fine, Uncle Vern!" I said, "It's real good."

I did not want him attempting any more of his Doctor ABCs and what he called cardio-pulmonary resurrection on me again. I was fully prepared to spray him in the eyes with my puffer if necessary.

"OK," he said, "But if you have the slightest shortness of breath you let me know at once because I have done the first aid course with the Brotherhood of St Laurence."

"Yes, Uncle Vern," I said.

"Good. Do you remember Teresa?" Uncle Vern asked.

"Teresa who, Uncle Vern?"

"Teresa Green, Reg. You know, Teresa who was up at Big Flat Creek Track that time with Great-great-grandad Rodney and Roy Grogan and old Cyril Mustard. I told you all about it."

I couldn't help myself ejaculating,

"Oh, no, Uncle Vern, please! Not another bad story!"

A look of total mortification came over Uncle Vern's face.

"Bad story!!" he exclaimed in disbelief and outrage. "BAD STORY!!!"

He went a liverish colour and there was a hint of aggression about him as he grabbed the front of my pyjamas in his big claw and wrenched me up from the bedclothes. His eyes bulged and I could see his nose veins throbbing as he held my face so close, so awfully close to his. I felt myself in danger of becoming an instant alcoholic and my gorge rose suddenly. I was overcome and began to cry. This seemed to calm him down.

"Well, since you put it that way, Reg," he said, almost apologetically. "I'm sorry Reginald, if you're not feeling up to it then..." he said as he lowered me again. and he looked furtively down the front of my pyjamas. "Heavens above! Why Reginald! You're getting chest hairs! Well done, Reggie! See, that's the good country life for you. You old devil, all this time you've been holding out on us. Just wait till I tell your Auntie Mona!"

I felt relieved, but ashamed.

"Reg," said Uncle Vern, "alls what I was trying to say before was that I had hoped that you would realize that while sometimes in these stories I tell you there might be some bad things happen - women doing the wrong thing, men making mistakes and suchlike - the thing is that these stories that I am telling you are moral stories, as moral as, as, as moral as God himself. Far more moral than the stuff they try to peddle in Sunday School. Ask them in Sunday School who Noah's sons married! What about that one who did it with his daughters in the cave! Both of them! Lot, him's the boy. They did it to him. They got him drunk and took it in turns! His own flesh and blood daughters did that to him. What did Mary Magdalene do for a living? What about Cain and Abel? A vegetarian was the first murderer! Never trust a vegetarian Greenie, Reg. Not that I am saying the Bible isn't true, no, but there are unanswered questions. Over all that time a few pages have to go missing, eh?

"The thing is, Reg, that you are becoming a man whether you like it or not. A man, Reggie! A man! And you must know what men are. You must know what men can do. You must know to what depths a man can plunge, so you can plunge to those depths, too! So that you can plunge to those depths and preserve mankind as we know it. This is a holy office, Reg. Teresa, after all, was named after a saint. No matter how far men get out into the bush these basic, spiritual instincts never leave them. Never!

"The difference between good and bad is a far from straightforward matter, Reg. Even angels and saints can go wrong, son, so what hope is there for mortal country people to lead a blameless life? None whatever. It is in the very nature of people to be wicked. That is why forgiveness and understanding are always necessary. That is the importance of Jesus, Reg. God the Father lays down the law and fiercely punishes the transgressors, and Jesus the Son forgives and comforts. It's just like the nasty policeman and the nice one, Reg, exactly the same."

It was unusual, and slightly disturbing for me, to hear Uncle Vern to dwell at such length on religious matters. Auntie Mona had mentioned that lately Uncle Vern had taken to seeing a somewhat unorthodox preacher who had taken up an itinerancy in the district. Instinctively I had little faith that it could lead to any good. Religious movements came and went in the district like other fads. Atheists became Born Again Christians became Methodists became Buddhists became In and Outers (see Uncle Vern Story # 12 'Bull's Wedding' - Ed). I never thought Uncle Vern, who had lapsed from a stern Baptist heritage, would take such things seriously.

I gazed out the window, wondering where such a development could lead. Uncle Vern seemed to read my thoughts.

"I know what you're thinking, Reg. You shouldn't be surprised. Country people are religious. They have to be. Every second year is bad and every third a disaster. It's a hard life, Reg, people need something to fall back on. Some people just fall back on the dirt, but others find they need more. Young Roy's people were like that.

"Young Roy's father and mother were battlers, Reg, real battlers. His mother, Gloria, God rest her soul, had suffered fearfully from polio and as a little girl she had had to be pushed around in a little trolley. By dint of sheer willpower she had taught herself to walk with the aid of a stick, but she could never dance so she was out of the way of courting and by the age of twenty-two she was well on the way to becoming an old maid. That was when she met Hector, Roy's father.

"Hec Grogan was a good man basically, but raised in the bush and rough about the edges. He had about him a natural exuberance that led to bouts with the bottle, but as you often find with drinkers he had a feeling for idealism and could get very sentimental, very prone to feelings of pity. That's how he felt whenever he saw her, Gloria, being pushed along in the trolley.

"He used to say that someone should marry that poor girl and show her what a good happy home life could be. But he knew her people would never accept him, and he was right.

"Now, Gloria's people, the Mountbanks, were well-off people. They had a tractor and a front paddock full of roses and a radio, everything. They looked right down their long noses at people like Hec, and when he managed to raise the courage to ask them for the hand of their daughter he was laughed off the property.

"Gloria was heartbroken, but not defeated. She escaped from her room one night and hobbled - she had almost learnt to walk by then - all the way, fifteen miles, to Hec's little place on the leased swamp he was reclaiming in order to start a prickly pear farm. There, in the dawnlight, they were wed in the old bush way.

"When her parents found out they disowned her and never spoke to her again. The marriage was happy. They had four children in four years and all of them survived. Hec worked hard draining the swamp and the prickly pears proliferated. They didn't always have enough money for food but they could always get by on kangaroo and nardoo seeds and bardi grubs and they got by.

"But then everything went wrong. First, Gloria conceived twins. Then the government declared the prickly pear a noxious weed. Five floods in five months refilled the swamp. Gloria died giving birth to young Roy and Roylene. And, after all that, Hec took to the bottle in a serious way.

"Can you imagine what it was like for poor Hec? Broke, living in a swamp full of prickly pears with six kids under six, and a serious drinking problem, nine miles from the pub and his only transport a bicycle with threadbare tyres.

"There was no light whatsoever at the end of the tunnel, nor along the road from the pub where he regularly crashed his bike and broke his arms. He was drinking and bicycling himself to death. The kiddies were neglected and forced to beg for food and clothes, though they were good, polite kids and they kept the show together while Hec was the scandal of the district.

"Then his salvation came. One night he was riding home when he fell of his bike and landed facefirst in the gravel. There is the moonlight as he lay recovering his senses he saw something that changed his life. It was Jesus's face in the gravel, smiling up at him. He was struck by blessedness, and there and then he gave up the bottle and became the fiercest, most moralistic, wowserist Christian that ever terrorised a country town this side of Mecca.

"He set to work rebuilding his life. He got clothes for the kids, he worked as a day labourer and fruit picker, renewed his work draining the swamp, and he made sure the kids learnt to read and write so they could read the bible and write away for more tracts which they used to distribute in their spare time.

"Gradually he built the place up. He bought eight old huts from the Country Roads Board, as it was called then. They all had one each and one was the kitchen. The motherless family was starting to live in a civilized manner. But the kids went funny. Young as they were, while he was drunk, they managed everything . Later, however, when he took charge again, for some reason they rebelled against the religion, and started running wild.

"There seemed to be no end to the bad luck that could befall Hec Grogan. They say no man in this district ever worked harder than Hec once he had the fear of God in him. He made big plans. He was going to build a chapel amidst a Garden of Eden in the reclaimed swamp but then one day he was standing under a gum tree in a storm and he got struck by lightning and died.

"More or less straightaway the older kids cleared off and they have never been seen back here again and Roy and Roylene were left alone with the eight shacks and two graves and an enormous pile of firewood. For some months Roylene ran wild and she became known as the town bike and as a bad influence.

"Young Roy was sort of lost and in a way has spent the rest of his life trying to replace his Dad. Well, life went on after a fashion for some time. Roy just moped about the swamp. Roylene fed him . She always seemed to manage to get some money from somewhere. But then, when the firewood their father had left them had almost run out, she left too. It was then that Young Roy took up with Cyril and Great-Grandad Rodney.

"For a time the huts in the swamp were abandoned, but Roy always returned there and until he died it was his set.

"We know all about Roy's adventures in the bush, but we did not hear nothing of Roylene for many years, nearly ten years, ten long years it was before she was heard of again. That was when she came back from the city. Being Roy's twin we remembered her as his double, except she was a girl, and lacked his short hair and wore different clothes and so forth.

"But the city had changed her, Reg and when she came back she was his spitting image. Roy had wavy blond hair slicked back like Elvis, and now she did too. They both wore riding boots and jeans, checked flannel shirts and denim jackets. They both had a cigarette sticking out of their mouths and they both had whiskers, not a lot of whiskers, but a few. Roy had always had a high sort of voice and now

Roylene's had dropped somewhat and the people in the hotel were amazed that they couldn't tell the two of them apart. It was even said that at times they could not tell themselves who they were.

"You can imagine the confusion and laughs they had as a result of their incredible similarity. It was very hard on some of the blokes who remembered Roylene fondly from the old days when she used to be such a good sport. They kept trying her out but they kept getting Roy. It seemed uncanny how often they were wrong until one day Roy let it be known that Roylene had confided in him that she no longer recognized men in the biblical sense.

"Nevertheless this didn't stop some of them, blokes trying to see if they could remind her and possibly persuade her to reconsider this unfortunate new approach she had to life. Yes, they had no shortage of guests coming out to the swamp to help them drink, but most of these guests found themselves in the way somewhat as Roy and Roylene grappled with many thorny family issues that had preyed on their minds for years.

"So the hopeful visitors usually had to sit through hours and hours of unresolved family disputes between the twins and none could manage to stay up long enough to try it out on Roylene.

"That is, except for young Andrew, the barman at the hotel, who was just a cut cleverer than most of the men in the district. He went out there and tried to make small talk but of course Roy and Roylene began their arguing and he couldn't get a word in so he pretended to be completely done in and retired early.

"' You can sleep in my shack, Andrew, if you like,' said Young Roy.

"' Thanks, mate!' said Andrew and off he went with his beer, candle and mosquito coil and he laid himself down on Roy's stinking little cot and waited, watching the light in the kitchen shack and hearing the distant sounds of their continual arguments.

"On and on they argued into the night. Young Andrew dozed off a few times and he was in fact asleep when they finally called it a night.

"As usual, the night drew to a close when they ran out of beer. Their long arguments did not result in bitterness, they were twins after all, and when Roylene mentioned that she thought Andrew might pay her a call later in the night, and that she might like to let Roy sleep in her bed and she would sleep in the kitchen, Young Roy readily agreed. Thus they called it a night.

"An hour later Young Andrew awoke with a start. The light in the kitchen was off. There was a faint light coming from Roylene's shack. The sounds of heavy snoring filled the air. Instantly he slithered from the bed and made his way to Roylene's shack. "

"' Roylene? ' he said cautiously, to make sure she was asleep, for the element of surprise was vital, 'Roylene, are you awake?'

"There was no answer. He crept inside. The Tilley lamp was down real low. Roylene was lying face down on the bed fast asleep, or so he thought. For how was he to know that they had swapped huts? Unaware of this cruel trick of fate he rolled her over slightly and undid her belt and jeans and pulled them down. She had done this very thing many times in the old days, he knew from the older men in the bar, and she wouldn't mind at all...

"Rough as he was, Young Andrew did not wake the sleeping body. Though the thing was more difficult than he had expected, he satisfied himself as quickly and as quietly as possible and then prepared to quit the scene. Being something of a young gentleman he pulled 'her' jeans back up so that in the morning nothing would be amiss. But just as he had finished doing this the body, Roy, stirred.

"' Zat you Andrew? ' said young Roy sleepily.

"'Yeah.'

"' You after beer?'

"' Yeah.'

"' We drank it.'

"' Oh,' said Andrew. ' Any tobacco left?'

"' Stove.' said Roy, not aware of nothing.

"' Thanks,' said Andrew, and he stole away into the night, thinking that he had just been talking with Roylene. He did not bother hanging about because he had spent long enough in Roy's cot already, so he picked his way home through the prickly pears, quietly pleased with himself. In fact the next day he let the matter slip at the hotel. The other men, who had long ago given up on Roylene, were suitably impressed at least for the time being.

"But as they say, son, truth will out. The next morning Roy experienced a great deal of pain and a persistent discharge and as the discharge did not stop by lunchtime he went for the doctor. The doctor was not sure what it was but sent a specimen of the discharge off for testing and applied a suitable poultice.

"A week later when the doctor found out what it was he simply told Roy that he had had an attack of albumen and that it wasn't nothing to worry about.

"Now I know what you're thinking, Reg, that the doctor had a duty to be discreet about these things, and indeed he has and he asked me not to tell anyone about this business - what good would it do anyone to know the truth? - None! - so I must ask you too not to tell anyone what you know."

I promised not to tell a word.

"The reason I tell you this Reg is to let you know that a man can sin without even realizing that he is doing anything wrong at all. It does not have to be his fault, but still he sins. You can't be too careful, Reg. The Almighty has set traps for the unwary everywhere. It is a very hard world."

THE SIXTY-NINER

a poignant memoir of war

An Uncle Vern Story: External Use only

Auntie Mona had gone down to Polo's Daytrap Bridge Autoport Cafe for a cappuccino. She did this two or three times a week and it seemed to relax her. But with Uncle Vern it was the usual, unrelenting work.

Uncle Vern and I were down in the top paddock checking to see if Desmond the bull had been on the job.

"Good old Diane!" said Uncle Vern as he slid his arm inside her as far as it would go. The cows had been skittish that morning and Uncle Vern had had to approach most of them on all fours and from downwind but dear old Diane had had her lobotomy the previous autumn and she would placidly put up with almost anything. Vern sweated and grunted as he groped around inside the animal. Diane chewed her cud contentedly.

"I can't feel anything, Reg," he said at length as he tenderly withdrew his arm. "People will try to tell you all sorts of malarkey about the country life, Reg, but I am here to tell you it is a tough, arduous, bump and grind. It is not for the weak or the squeamish or the faint of heart!"

He took a good, long sniff at the crook of his elbow. He placed several fingers inside his nostrils and inhaled deeply. He licked the palm of his hand and swilled the mucus around in his mouth thoughtfully and then spat it out. "It is tough and demanding," he said fiercely, "and I love it. Some farmers swallow that stuff, but I don't. Desmond has been on the job, Reg, but he has been firing blanks."

We still had seventy-three more cows to check but Uncle Vern said suddenly, "Damn it all, Reg, let's go yabbying!" I groaned inwardly. This undoubtedly meant another of his dreadful tales. He was already stalking to the dam.

"But Uncle Vern," I cried desperately, "we haven't got any meat!"

Uncle Vern turned and said, somewhat pompously, "Vern always has meat!"

By the time I got to the yabbying spot Uncle Vern had his boots off. He pulled some wool from his jumper and tied lengths of it to each of his suppurating socks.

"Here's yours!" he said.

I accepted the thing in silence and threw it into the algae. I pushed it down with a stick. Vern cracked open his thermos of slivovitz and chickory and was already rubbing his shag. Having lit his smoke, he pulled his pocketknife out of its belt pouch and began to whittle on a bit of river wood.

"The Revolution!" he said, bitterly. "You kids of today know nothing. The streetfighting in Stalingrad was a doddle - a doddle - compared with some of the things I saw!"

Though Uncle Vern had accumulated many wounds and injuries and illnesses in his life he had not actually been in a war as such. His membership of the Wallabong RSL was only an associate membership.

Uncle Vern was born too late for the last big stoush with the hated Hun and the cruel Jap. He was too late for Korea, too, and, though he had tried to enlist for Vietnam he was, amazingly, rejected on grounds of chronic piles and general deficiency. Nevertheless his life had not been untouched by great conflict.

And like many an old soldier he was wont to discourse on the great struggle which had stolen the best years of his youth and manhood and which had left many scars on his mind and body.

I tried to say something to divert him but he over-rode me.

"Don't try to gainsay me, Reg. For years I was caught in the vicious crossfire, lost in no-man's land. I was a volunteer..."

Tears were welling in his eyes.

"Sorry, Reg, but whenever I think of my fallen comrades...they were so young...so innocent...so fit..."

He sobbed.

"Forgive me, Reg, life has done this to me!"

I looked away.

"Reginald," he said, gathering his composure, " I know that of which I speak. But it is impossible to tell anyone who did not see active service in the Sexual Revolution what it was like! Try to tell young people today about glory boxes, six o'clock closing, the shotgun wedding, car key parties, maiden aunts and droit de seigneur and they laugh at you in disbelief."

"I believe you, Uncle Vern," I lied.

"Yes, I know you do, Reg, you're a good lad. I mean the average youth and pre-teenager in the pinball parlour, or at the dodgem cars or hanging around public conveniences, they have no idea. I am going to tell you a story Reg, and I am sorry, but you will find things out that will shock you deeply. You must never try any of the things you hear about in this sad saga. Do you know what a hippy girl is, Reg?"

"Not really, Uncle Vern," I said.

"In years gone by, Reg, we didn't have all the single parent families and lesbians and homeless children that you have nowadays. We had maiden aunts and orphanages. To be honest, Reg, I can't tell you which way was better - some of those maiden aunts were tough to live with. It's all different now. We won the war, and lost the peace. Where did we go wrong?"

Uncle Vern's attention had drifted again. A crow flapped past us laboriously. Uncle Vern threw his knife into the dam. Then, realizing that he still had the bit of wood, he angrily threw that in as well.

"Getting on for twenty-five years ago when the Sexual Revolution, the great battle between the sexes and generations, raged back and forth across the country, dividing families and tearing small rural communities asunder, there was a young man in this district who foolishly believed that you could bring all people together to live in harmony. He was a very good friend of mine. Do you know what a sleeper is, Reg?"

"A person who sleeps, Uncle Vern?"

"An undercover agent, Reg. A deep cover agent. I cannot tell you his name because even to this day it remains classified information by court order, but let us call him Craig. We were both undercover agents. We were sixty-niners. I don't suppose you know what a sixty-niner is, Reg, but for your information those of us who volunteered in 1969 were known as sixty-niners. We joined up in the early days of unisex salons.

Craig's mission was to infiltrate the roaming bands of hippy shock troops who were fanning out across the countryside, duping and brainwashing and sponging off of innocent, hard-working, decent, clean-living country folk.

Craig lived at the time on a small farmlet not far from Daytrap when in the summer of 1969 a distinctive bus pulled into the caravan park.

This was no ordinary bus. It was all done up like a pox doctor's clerk. It was psychotic. The bus was completely covered with flowers and eyes and butterflies, leaves, mushrooms, mystic symbols and way out patterns. The sides of the bus were adorned with the words 'Free Love' and 'Make Love Not War'. The front of the bus had been painted like a face and the destination scroll had been turned to where someone had painted the word, 'Nowhere'. Nothing like it had ever been seen in these parts before.

"Now as you are aware, Reg, we live in the freest country in the entire free world. We have the finest sense of humour known to man and we make the best beer. In other words we are the most tolerant country there ever was - we are tolerant to a fault.

"An ordinary, right thinking person would be content with that. But there are those among us who would abuse their privileges, flaunt their freedoms, who live on the dole and take drugs and would destroy our way of life.

"Inside that bus there were such people, Reg, the enemies of normality. Free Love, Reg, is the greatest lie that was ever invented to try the patience of man. Try asking about free love in Kings Cross and see where it gets ya! It was their evil mission to spread the twin doctrines of free love and peace across the country like so much poison honey across an enormous slice of toast, smothering the very fabric of our democratic way of life. They can talk about free love until it turns blue, but will they act on it? No way! And peace be blowed. I will tell you this once, Reg: never ever turn your back on a pacifist. There are very good reasons why men wear trousers and women wear dresses, Reg. Biological reasons. Social Reasons. Practical reasons. "

I sensed that this story was going nowhere.

"Shouldn't we check the yabbies, Uncle Vern, "I asked.

"No, Reg, not yet. The yabbies in this pond are extremely cunning. You must give them time. Besides, we haven't got a bucket.

"Agent Craig investigated. He drove his ute to the caravan park on the pretext of seeing old Cyril Mustard. Cyril at the time had been brain dead for some years so Craig just sat with him in the guest chair outside the annexe, occasionally adjusting his cigarette butt and mopping up from time to time the spittle that gathered in the folds of Cyril's neck and cheek dewlaps, and talking to him. It was good to talk to old Cyril.

"The bus was the only other vehicle in the park at the time and before long Craig noticed some movement. There were three women. They had long hair and beads and they wore tight jeans that looked like they had been painted on with watercolours. He watched as two of the girls hung out a clothes line and then they hung their clothes out on the clothes line.

"For the first time in his life Craig saw tie-dyed T-shirts and embroidered frocks with elephants and bells and mirrors on 'em. He also noticed baby clothes though there was no sign of any men.

"Craig himself was the epitome of country taste and style. He wore a pair of highly buffed R.M.Williams boots - riding boots - and Levi Longhorn jeans without underpants. He had a navy Chesty Bonds singlet under his red-checked Miller shirt without the tassles but with mother-of-pearl buttons. Above the open-necked shirt he wore a turquoise bandana and his head was crowned with a burgundy Stetson 'Big Run'. His thumbs were tucked inside his belt either side of the big V8 buckle when one of the hippy girls approached him and said,

"'Hi!'"

"'How're ya goin'?' he said, laconically.

"Just like a bushman, he knew that they would notice him and be irresistibly attracted to him.

"She was real pretty, and young. Young and pretty.

"'You from 'round here?' she asked.

"'I might be,' said Craig, 'I get around.'

"He knew he could not give too much away to the enemy.

"'What's your name?' she asked, real friendly like.

Craig was alert.

"'My name is Vern,' he said

"I can never forgive him for that," said Uncle Vern, " but I realize why he had to do it. He had to think quickly, and it is not surprising that he should think of his best mate's name before anything else is it?"

"No, Uncle Vern," I said.

"'My name is Dewdrop,' she said.

"' That's a nice name, Dewdrop,' said Craig.

"'Far out,' said Dewdrop, 'Crazy threads!'

That meant she liked his clothes. Craig's heart beat violently. She was obviously touched; she was on the other side; she was probably on drugs, too; and yet there was something about her.

"Craig had feelings then that would later lead him into the dark, smokey world of double entendres. Young Craig, an upright country man, would have run a thousand miles rather than be taken for a double entendre, but that was his dreadful fate. Yet how could he have suspected anything as his gaze rested upon this sweet smiling flower child?

"'Maybe you could help me...' she said.

"She began to ply her feminine wiles.

"'What's the problem ?' said Craig with a suggestion of amusement in his voice as if there was no such thing as a problem when he was around. He knew women like manly capability, that they felt good with it around and that by using it and exuding it he would win their confidence.

"'Our stove is smokey,' said Dewdrop.

"'Prob'ly the flue,' said Craig, 'Wouldja like me to look at it for ya?'

"' Well, if you're not too busy...' she said

"'Well I was planning on filing me nails this morning, but I guess I could put it off until later..' said Agent Craig by way of a joke. Dewdrop giggled and led the way to their mobile home.

"When he stepped into the weird bus it was like stepping into another world. The place smelled like roses of attar. There were pictures of freaky people with guitars and negroes. A parachute hung from the ceiling. In the middle of the bus was a pot-bellied stove. The crazy twanging of Indian music filled the air. At the far end of the bus the other two girls were engrossed over a layout of strange cards. One of them was feeding a baby at her breast. Agent Craig was shocked and fascinated and even touched by this scene. The two girls smiled and nodded to him as his manly form entered.

"' That's Crystal and that's Vyvyan' said Dewdrop. 'This is Vern, he has come to fix the stove,' she explained.

"Agent Craig went to the stove. He saw the problem at once. The damper was closed. He opened it and said, 'There ya go, you can have a real good fire now. Once it's going you can turn it down like this, see.'

"'Do you know anywhere we might get some firewood?' asked Dewdrop.

"When he got back an hour later with two tons of red box firewood she let him try some of her homemade soup. It was most unusual, and he complimented her on it and asked what it might be. It was made from lentils and patchouli oil. Then he fixed three flat tyres and tuned the bus. By the time he had finished these jobs he was fairly stuffed and it was still only midday but he knew he had to stick with it.

"Craig was racked with doubt. He realized that they were the enemy and that he should report their activities to the authorities and yet he felt increasingly attracted to them, especially the quiet one, the prettiest one, Vyvyan. So far he had not compromised himself, but soon he would be tested.

"'Let's go skinnydipping!' said Dewdrop.

"Craig was shocked. 'Sure,' he said. He was on the tiger's back now and he dared not get off. Dewdrop began to remove her sandals...

"'Wait!' cried Agent Craig, 'you can't do that here, I mean the shop is just over there, I mean...'

"'What's wrong with you, Craig, you big square,' she said. 'It's cool, this is a free country, isn't it?'

"'But, er, I mean the water is too shallow here. I know a real good spot, not too far from here, we can go in my ute. You can dive in and all.'

"'Far out,' said Dewdrop. ' I'll go and get Vyvyan.'

"Moments later she came back from the bus and said that Vyvyan was going to stay and look after the baby and have a nap.

"Craig was disappointed but did not complain. They all piled into his ute and as he slipped her into gear Craig realized that he had a serious problem.

"He had never been skinnydipping before, though he knew what was involved. It was the same problem that had for many years prevented him from joining a nudist colony. The waterhole was ten kilometres away and all the way there he sweated nerves and hardly spoke at all because his mental powers were busy driving and trying to relax. The girls seemed not to notice and chatted happily.

"Quietly he slipped off his shoes as he drove. He had an idea. When he got there he would leap from the vehicle as if he were water crazy and run to the pool. As long as he had his back to them the water might do the trick.

"When he pulled up at the old fireplace he leapt from the car hootin' and hollerin' and he ran, tearing his clothes off, to the rockpool. Just as he took off for his dive he realized that if he did a normal dive the jig would be up so at the last moment he arched his back and sort of fell into the water like an oaf.

"The girls laughed at this and Craig laughed too, with relief. The cold, clear, mountain water began to work. It was hardly instantaneous, but it was a definite improvement. But then the girls began to take their clothes off.

"There was a great charm in the way they did it, a simplicity that was wed by the sunlight to the naturalness of the bush. A kingfisher darted. Bellbirds carolled. The great, white trunks of the red river gums gleamed brightly; river dragons lazed on rocks unafraid of the humans; the heady scent of eucalyptus hung heavy in the still summer air. Dewdrop's firm, full breasts jiggled slightly as she slipped out of her panties and Crystals did the same, perhaps a little more emphatically and despite the cold, clear mountain water Craig's manhood was harder than granite. And yet his teeth were chattering like a cage full of monkeys. The girls did not jump into the water at once. Instead they sat on the diving rock and began to roll a cigarette, the biggest cigarette Craig had ever seen.

"Crystal called to Craig.

"' Hey man, wanna smoke?'

"Agent Craig accepted the large smoke, not knowing that it contained the infamous sex-drug marijuana. He puffed on it deeply as he had seen the girls doing. It only took that one puff and he was gone. He puffed again. Already he was addicted. He had a third puff, and a fourth.

"'Hey Craig, man, how about giving us a smoke?' said Dewdrop. ' We take it in turns, you know. It's called sharing.'

"Backing towards them , for the sexdrug had made his manhood even more troublesome, he held up the smoke. They took it. Agent Craig noticed a grasshopper at the edge of the pool. He looked at it very, very closely. Suddenly he heard all the sounds of the bush at once. The grasshopper was waving its arms, or legs or whatever they were. As if by a miracle, Craig realized that the bush was like a big orchestra with the wind in the trees, the birds, the timber trucks on the highway, they were all part of a great symphony and this little grasshopper that he just happened to notice was conducting the whole lot. It was all a bit much. He had never felt like this before.

"Splash! The girls dove into the water. As they surfaced Agent Craig noticed that their nipples were standing up stiffly like soldiers outside Buckingham Palace. He began to giggle. ' The little grasshopper is conducting the orchestra!' he said.

"'Yeah, sure man.' said the girls. They laughed. Their laughter was cruel and conspiratorial.

"Agent Craig knew that his duty was to insinuate himself into their organisation as far as possible, even if it meant being intimate with them. They were naked and obviously available. The time was right, yet his natural morality held him back. And there was his girlfriend, Jackie, to think of. Jackie had left to see her cousin in Melbourne five years ago and he had promised to be faithful and wait for her return. Agent Craig was a man of his word.

"'You OK, Craig?' the girls called, for he had seemed to them strangely quiet. He had to think. It was hard, and it made thinking hard, too.

"'Yeah.' said Craig.

"His enormous sense of duty fought an epic battle with his unshakeable country modesty. There were times when they splashed around, apparently innocently (though Craig knew that they knew perfectly well that they knew what they were doing, the glances, the little giggles, they knew the game) there were times when he almost jumped on one or both of them but he could not. After a desperately tense fifteen minutes they climbed out of the pool and lay on their backs on the grass and wiggled their toes. Their firm young breasts - Crystal's bursting with sweet, human milk - pointed up to the clear summer sky.

"His sense of duty was unbearably strong but every time he tried to act upon it the image of his mother would appear before him to remind him of his natural sense of propriety.

"They began to put their clothes on. They beautiful flesh was disappearing beneath the hated hippy garments. Agent Craig sensed that this could be his last chance slipping away. His soldier's instincts told him that he had to act and act quickly.

"Not caring for his own safety he leapt from the pool, his manhood rearing and bucking like a rodeo bull as he lunged first at Dewdrop and then at Crystal, then at Dewdrop and then at Crystal again. The hippy girls knew that the jig was up. They fully realized what they were dealing with and that they had no chance against his righteousness so they did the cowardly thing and they ran screaming into the bush. Their lissom young bodies slipped into the undergrowth and disappeared. The main reason they got away was their tight jeans.

"Instinctively Agent Craig got into his ute and drove at breakneck speed back to the caravan park. He would have the pretty girl, the quiet one. She had had about her an innocent look, an honest look. She was young and alluring. In all probability she was not really a hippy at all and she would worship him for having saved her from the clutches of the counter culture.

"Still affected by the pernicious sex-drug marijuana he burst into the hippy bus and went for Vyvyan. But Vyvyan, though terrified, was quick and agile as a young girl on heat. She ran for the door. Craig grabbed her by the jeans But she broke free. In a sexy, husky voice she said coyly, 'Let me go!' This only served to fire up Agent Craig even more.

"She ran across the caravan park and up the hill and over the bridge and into the downtown area of Daytrap. Craig, crazed by drugs and his sense of duty, forgetting, tragically, that he was birthday naked, chased her like a man possessed.

"People came from the hotel and the shop and Polo's autoport when they heard Vyvyan's cries for help.

"Voices cried out to Agent Craig. 'Vern, it's a man! Vern, it's a man!' I mean 'Craig, it's a man! Craig, it's a man!'

"Someone appeared with a blanket. Agent Craig was kinghit from behind in the interests of country propriety. They did not realize the battle he was fighting on their behalf. They were sadly ignorant in those days. It was a hard thing.

"Agent Craig was cashiered and had to leave the district.

"In the fullness of time the complete story came out of how he had been drugged and duped. But by then the hippies were long gone.

"Agent Craig eventually returned to the district in his own good time some three months later. The people were apologetic. He was accorded a hero's welcome and he generously consented to settle in the district again, though he has always, since then, because of his combat trauma, been sparing in his public appearances."

Uncle Vern pointed to the dam. Hundreds and hundreds of yabbies had floated to the surface.

"Not a bad catch," he said.

"Good heavens, Uncle Vern," I exclaimed, "Are they dead?"

"Some are dead, Reg, but the majority are simply comatose. They will remain that way as long as we leave the bait in. That gives you time to go and get a bucket. I shall wait here and make sure they do not try to escape. Hurry on, Reg, and bring my spare thermos back with you," he said, taking another life giving swig on the slivovitz.

As I walked back to the farm I racked my brain to think of a way to avoid having to eat any of the noxious catch, because I knew to do so would mean certain death. Uncle Vern called to me before I was out of earshot.

"Reg!"

"Yes, Uncle Vern?"

"Do you understand now why women wear dresses and men wear trousers? The lie of the Sexual Revolution was to enable women to wear trousers as part of the trade off for so-called free love. They got control of a deadly weapon, and we got nothin'! This is high politics, Reg, and it's not over yet."

"Okay, Uncle Vern," I yelled back, "Don't worry, I'll get it."

THE SPIRITED FLESH

passion beyond the grave

An Uncle Vern Story: Enter At Own Risk

It was a hard winter morning. White frost bristled in the paddocks. A sharp wind cut at our scarves like a dull razor. I was on the trailer with the Stanley knife and hay. Uncle Vern was driving the tractor and singing "She Wears My Ring" in his fiercest voice. The cows were following along behind us picking up the leaves of hay as I peeled then from the bales.

The tractor slowed, then stopped. Uncle Vern got down and walked to a thing on the ground. It was a calf, a dead calf. Uncle Vern shook his head. He kicked it gently.

"Poor thing," he said. "It's dead."

He went back to the tractor and brought back a jerry can of diesel and a funnel. He poured the diesel liberally over the little corpse. The mother cow stood at a distance lowing pathetically. Uncle Vern shoved the funnel into the dead thing's mouth and said to me,

"Reggie, hold this for me will you!"

I did so and he poured in diesel until it ran back out the mouth.

"Okay," said Uncle Vern. Then he began trying to light it with matches. He tried and tried but it wouldn't go. Finally he said, "It's just as well I ate those left over cabbage rolls this morning. I'll show you how they used to do this in the old days!" Then, to my amazement, he dropped his trousers and squatted over the thing the way sprinters settle into their blocks. He applied a lighted match to his underpants and suddenly there was a velvet roar as a blue flame leapt and flickered and poured over the diesel-soaked body. After a few seconds it was blazing nicely. He tied up his trousers as he remounted the tractor.

"Come on Reg," he said, "let's get on with it!"

Back at the toolshed Uncle Vern mentioned that Auntie Mona was planning to go to the dancing class at the Daytrap Hall that evening. I said I was thinking of accompanying her.

"Don't be silly, Reggie. Dancing is for girls!" he said as he limped around the trailer with the broom, sweeping it carefully. " On dance nights able-bodied men stand outside the hall and drink beer and yarn and keep an eye out for trouble. You'd be far better off staying here tonight where you might learn something educational. I have something very special planned for this evening! Visitors are coming, Reg!"

This was indeed unusual.

People were rarely entertained after dark at Uncle Vern and Auntie Mona's farm. Partly this was because they were early to rise and early to retire, and partly because the people of the district seemed not to socialize with each other very often. But even if they had been inclined to receive guests in the evenings, the bizarre, alcohol-induced, personality changes that Uncle Vern underwent after seven pm mitigated against it.

I wondered what it could be.

"We are going to make contact with the other side, Reginald," said Uncle Vern.

"What, Uncle Vern?" I said.

"The other side, Reg! The spirit world! Doctor Who is coming with his ouija board. Polo is coming too, and Dick Katz. Do you know what today is?"

"Friday, Uncle Vern," I said confidently.

"No, no, Reg, the date."

"August..." I ventured.

"The sixteenth, Reg. August the Sixteenth. The King, Reg, this is the day the King died. There are those who say that he is working at a service station in Nevada and has amnesia; there are those who say that he is a saintly man running a leper colony in Paraguay; or a sheltered poolroom for single mothers with breast cancer in Hoboken, New Jersey; or that the Chinese took him by submarine to be boiled down for aphrodisiacs; nice thoughts, Reg, nice thoughts, but they are only the prayers of hopeless people: we must face facts: the King Is Dead! Tonight we shall call him up on the ouija board. The Doctor can do it, he can do anything!"

"Gee!" I said. It sounded like it might be an interesting evening.

All that day Uncle Vern was in the toolshed alone. The sound of Elvis's music came from his stereophonic record player within: 'Jailhouse Rock', 'Crawfish', 'Return To Sender', 'Wooden Heart' and 'In The Ghetto.' He would let no one inside and a strong smell of Old Spice aftershave surrounded the building. I helped Auntie Mona for a while and spent a couple of hours throwing sticks for Flaps the dog but most of the time I just wandered around being bored.

Auntie Mona and I dined alone because Uncle Vern was still in the toolshed. After dinner Auntie Mona prepared for the dancing class. She wore perfume and lipstick. In her new powder-blue dress and black, afro-style wig and with her teeth in she looked real pretty. I told her so and she nearly cried.

"Thank-you, Reginald," she said and she kissed me on the cheek.

Just then Uncle Vern came in and saw her doing this and gave us both a long, searching look. I noticed that Uncle Vern was wearing a full length overcoat buttoned to the top with a scarf and overshoes.

Auntie Mona said hopefully, "How do I look?" .

Uncle Vern looked at her and shook his head. "You look ridiculous," he said, "Absolutely ridiculous."

"Thank-you, Vern," she said coldly. "I might have expected a comment like that from you. Your dinner is in the oven. I am going out now and I shall be back late."

With that she walked out. I wiped off her kiss. Uncle Vern went to the oven muttering about 'mutton done up as lamb' and got out his dinner. He took it to the table covered it with tomato sauce and salt and wolfed it down. He looked at the clock. It said six-fifty-five. "Geez!" he exclaimed. "They'll be here in five minutes."

He picked up the table cloth by its corners, lifting with it all the dishes, and threw the lot into the linen press after taking out a heavy black cloth which he threw over the kitchen table. He rushed to the back porch and came back with arms full of aromatic oil evaporators and gave me a box of matches and told me to light them all. As I did so he shuttled back and forth to the verandah bringing into the room all manner of arcane objects - a goat's skull, an elaborate candelabra, a large star-like diagram with heirographic signs, the seed-pods of the date palm, a live guinea pig...the airhorn announced the arrival of Doctor Who at the gate.

"Strewth, they're here!" said Uncle Vern in alarm.

The air was filling with strange aromas, some pleasant, some not so pleasant, some downright foul.

Uncle Vern lugged in three slabs of beer and hurriedly hung posters of The King around the room. He had made an altar of the TV/Stereogram console. He ran to the bedroom and tore of his overshoes and coat and scarf and switched off the lights and threw me another box of matches.

"Light the candles!" he ordered.

As I lit the candles he turned off the lights. A haunting melody played on some pipelike instrument wafted in from the kitchen garden. Three shadowy figures approached. Polo was making the unearthly music. The deep voice of Doctor Who chanted in a strange language, and in the moonlight the short, stocky figure of Dick Katz swung before him a brazier.

"Thoth, cthnonium bok beryllium censor non disputandum de gustibus qui mal y pense, thoth beelzebub baal norks ..."

Amazed by this chilling imprecation I turned to see Uncle Vern standing before the makeshift altar resplendent in a red and black cape and beneath it he was a vision of sequins and tassels and acres of white satin. His hair was thick and luxuriant, like Elvis's, in fact he looked just like Elvis. He even had a couple of pillows stuffed into the white suit to give him the necessary bulk. Somewhere, very faintly, the old Elvis song, 'Crying In The Chapel' was playing. Uncle Vern was staring out like a zombie and holding a torch under his chin. The entire effect was terrifying and I began to wish that I had gone to the dancing lessons after all.

The sullen footfall of the three men without fell ominously on the verandah as they made their way around the outside of the entire house three times as Doctor Who chanted tenebrously, "Thoth, visigoth, stentor, sputum ecclesiasticus, horus lux, thoth baal, beelzebub, vathek..."

Then they stopped at the flyscreen door of the kitchen. The plangent strains of the piping stopped and the three men then chanted in unison.

"We are at the gate, O! Dark One!

Behold your acolytes, O Prince!

Accede to our desire, O Dark One!

E Pluribus Unum!

Admit us to the Sanctum!

Lillee! Lillee!

I had never seen adults behave in this way before, not even in a church.

"Enter my cohort of the night! "said Uncle Vern, sternly, from his altar.

The three men - all hooded - came in and chanted again.

"We are here to praise the King! "

Uncle Vern responded,

"You have done well, my brothers! Enter and partake of the sacrament. "

At this the three men relaxed somewhat. Polo put down his polypipe oboe, and Dick Katz put down his brazier. They took off their hoods and the Doctor covered the table with a large painted pane of glass he had been carrying and placed on it a champagne flute he took from from his pocket. They cracked open cans

of beer and Doctor Who warned them against
drinking over his ouija board.

"Drink over this board and I'll fuckin' kill ya! "he
said.

The ouija board was made from a submarine window.
The letters of the alphabet and the numbers one to ten
were arranged in a circle with the words 'yes' and 'no'
at opposite poles.

Before they had even drunk one beer Uncle Vern said,

"We'll have to get a wriggle on because Mona's gonna
be back around eleven! "

"You like my tarantella, Vern? "asked Polo.

"Very good, Polo, very unearthly, "said Uncle Vern.

"What have we got for a sacrifice? "asked Dick Katz,
adding," I've brought along Millane for the leftovers.
"

"We have a guinea pig, "said Uncle Vern.

"Is that all!? "said the Doctor.

"I'ma nota gonna cutta da heada offa him, "said
Polo," It'sa too harda to finda da necka. "

"No worries, Polo, ya stupid dago bastard, we can do
it in the microwave, "said Dick Katz.

"That's not a bad idea, Dick, "said the Doctor, adding," Have you prepared the magic potion, O grand-succubator Vern. "

"Yes, "said Uncle Vern," It is in the skull of Capricorn. Come, partake O faithful servants of Lo-Hocla. "

The men all took straws and gathered around the goat's skull and drank until it was all gone. I was excused from taking part because I was not yet old enough to drink. When they finished the other men fell back cursing Uncle Vern.

"Christ! Vern, that was a bit heavy on the Shellite, wasn't it? "said Dick Katz.

"Disgusting, "said Doctor Who.

"Itsa bad, but ita works, "said Polo.

And it was true. I have never seen men get drunk so fast. It was amazing to me that they still appeared to know what they were doing. Dick Katz fell to the ground with his eyes rolling back in their sockets. Doctor Who poured some beer on him, though, and he recovered pretty well, though he could not walk straight after that.

After drinking another beer they sat at the table of glass and put their fingers on the base of the upturned champagne flute. Then they sat looking at each other.

"Go on! "said Doctor Who.

"No, you do it, "said Uncle Vern.

"You do it, Vern, you're the Dark One's right hand man, aren't ya? "

"But.. "

"Go on, do it, "growled Doctor Who, somewhat impatiently.

"Hello? "enquired Uncle Vern in a weak little voice." Hello, is anyone out there? "

Even his own dog, Flaps, wouldn't have answered that. Actually Flaps never responded to him at all. He tried again.

"Is there anyone out there - on the other side, like - that wants to make contact with the living? I mean can anyone take a message to the spirit of the King, Elvis Presley? "

"What self-respecting spirit is going to answer a miserable effort like that, Vern? "

"Oh, well you do it, Doc, "said Uncle Vern, crestfallen though somewhat relieved.

"Well, first turn the music up a bit and you do your Elvis thing over there on the rug, I think that might help. Remember there's going to be a bit of competition for the King, tonight of all nights. "

Uncle Vern went to the gramophone and turned it up.

"Don' wanna be your tiger

'coz tigers play too rough.. "

Then he began to mime the song and mimic the hip thrusting, wriggling, gyrating style of the young Elvis. Dick and Polo were suitably impressed.

"Jesus H. Christ! "said Dick.

"What a Pakistani! "said Polo.

"I think the music should be a bit faster, "said Dick." Whaddaya reckon? Hang doggy, I'll fix it. "

He went to the gramophone and switched it to 45 rpm. Uncle Vern danced faster.

"Jeez, "said Dick," That Shellite mix sure gets ya going, doesn't it! Go Vernie, yeah baby! Go, "

Polo was clapping and staring at Uncle Vern in disbelief. His eyes were rolling somewhat. Doctor Who simply said,

"Bloody hell! "Then," Come on you blokes you're s'posed to have your fingers on the glass so we can call up the unliving. "

Then the Doctor began his incantation.

"We the living believers gathered by the stream at the place known to the eternals as The Footprint beseech ye shades to join with us and share your knowledge of all matters beyond the grave. Come, oh ye spirits! and set our hearts and minds at rest. We wish to know how fares The King, Elvis the Great of Memphis. Who will come and speak to us of Elvis? We have the living sacrifice in the microwave. We have burned the sacred unguents! We beseech thee! "

Doctor Who spoke with such conviction and such an air of authority that even Uncle Vern had stopped his frenzied dancing - which was not quite suited to 'Wooden Heart' even played at 45 rpm - and stared in mute terror. He sat at the table and placed his finger lightly on the champagne flute.

"By the Age of Thoth, uxor maximus fortunatis, sexus pinus longus.. "continued Doctor Who.

To my utter amazement the glass began to move. At first it was but a slight movement.

"Is someone there? "enquired Doctor Who.

The glass almost flew to 'yes'.

With that Polo appeared to faint.

"Is that a dead person? "asked Uncle Vern.

Once again the glass sped to 'yes'.

"Is there anything you want from us, the living? "asked Doctor Who of the spirit." Do you want the live sacrifice? "

The answer was again 'yes'.

"You must wait here for a minute, "said Doctor Who." Brother Lush will be here to attend you, O Spirit! "

Then Doctor Who and Dick Katz had a big argument about who was going to turn on the microwave which Dick settled by turning it on first. Doctor Who, disgruntled, said menacingly,

"Next time you come to my garage, Dick, I'm going to wreck your car! "

Meanwhile Uncle Vern who had at first been terrified of being left alone with the spirit, had begun to ask it some questions of his own.

"Are you a female spirit? "he asked.

There was a muffled bang as the little body of the guinea pig exploded in the microwave oven in a most disgusting manner.

"Yes, "replied the spirit.

"Are you pretty? "

The glass flew around the table, pointing to each letter as it spelled out the response,

"My bewty is spiritual. "

"Oh! "said Uncle Vern.

"Don't you molest that spirit, Vern, "said Doctor Who.

The other men rejoined the seance.

"Did ya like the live sacrifice? "asked Brother Katz.

The glass spelled out the words," Reel good. "

"Oh spirit, "said Doctor Who," can you now help us to locate the shade of the King, Elvis Presley? "

Once again the glass spun around the table with bewildering speed. With difficulty the men made out,

"I am looking for The King myself. I have been looking for him for many years. I want to make him mine. Love the King forever. I have found the King. "

"Where is he? Where is the King? "the men asked urgently. "Can you bring him to us?"

The spellbinding glass once more went around the table, but this time more slowly and the men could hardly believe what they saw.

"The King lives! "it said.

"Where? Where does the King live? "demanded Dick Katz.

"Please, Dick, don't speak to the spirits in a rough way. "scolded Vern.

Polo was snoring very erratically.

"Put a cushion on his head will you Reg, I can't hear myself think, "said Doctor Who, indicating Polo with his thumb.

Once again the glass moved.

"D . A . Y. T . R . A . P . "came the stunning reply.

And then without being spoken to the glass moved again.

"King, O King, take me and make me your Queen! "

All eyes were on Uncle Vern. Doctor Who was a picture of disbelief.

"It must be you, Vern, "he said.

The strange libation of Shellite and whatever else seemed to have rendered the men incapable of disbelief, or at least they were highly suggestible.

Uncle Vern might have been many things but he was not completely stupid.

"This is The King. "he said. Then he sang a bar of Heartbreak Hotel." I am here . Who is the spirit who wishes an audience with the King? "

The glass moved at once, but this time is was slowly, shyly, even coyly.

"Marilyn, "it said.

"Do you know anyone dead called Marilyn? "Dick asked Doctor Who. The Doctor shrugged his shoulders.

"Marilyn who? "asked Uncle Vern.

"Marilyn Monroe, "came back the amazing answer.

"I do not believe it! "declared Doctor Who. Uncle Vern looked most annoyed but then their attention was electrified by the sound of a small crash and the tinkle of breaking glass. They looked to the mantlepiece and saw that Uncle Vern's framed picture of Marilyn Monroe had fallen.

Uncle Vern ran to it.

"Oh, Marilyn, Marilyn, I'm sorry! That fool Doctor did not know what he was saying. He is but a mortal, he is not like us, forgive him, Marilyn my darling, my soul mate. "

And he kissed the portrait fervently as he hurried back to the ouija board.

"Marilyn, "said Uncle Vern," now that you have found the King at last, what would you like to do? "

"Everything! "came the instant reply.

"Do you think I'm sexy? "said Uncle Vern.

The glass seemed to struggle for a moment, as if it wanted to go to 'no' but finally it went to 'yes'.

                    An Uncle Vern Story: Enter At Own Risk

Doctor Who, seeming not to approve of this line of questioning, asked next,

"Where are you O Great Spirit of Marilyn? May we look upon you? "

"Yeah, and are ya wearing any clothes? "added Uncle Vern.

'Here', 'Yes' and 'No' were the answers. The next question was obvious.

Breathlessly we waited for the answer. The glass seemed reluctant to tell, but Uncle Vern forced her hand by saying" You do want to make love to the King, don't ya? "

"I am in the fridge, "replied Marilyn's spirit.

Doctor Who kicked open the fridge door.

"Where? "all three men asked at once.

"I have come back to earth, "replied the glass slowly," in the form of a jar of rollmops. "

This amazing announcement left the men somewhat at a loss. But not for long. Uncle Vern got the rollmops out of the fridge and set them by himself.

"Is that better? "he asked the spirit." Do you feel more at rest now that you are beside The King? "

"No, "came the reply." I am excited. It is too much. I cannot control my feelings. "

This was too much for Uncle Vern, too. With a growl he grabbed the jar of rollmops and headed for the door saying," I know how to open these bastards, "and he began to remove the lid by squeezing it between the door and the architrave.

I do not know for sure what happened next because I retreated to the outside toilet for a while. I heard sounds of protestation from Dick Katz and laughter from the Doctor and a bestial grunting and some bellowing. Dick left the house and ran down the drive.

The Doctor continued to laugh for some time. When quiet had returned I re-entered the house. There was even more debris around the place than I expected. The rollmops now sat on the ouija board and Uncle Vern was staring at it, unlikely as this may sound, lovingly. The sauce they were in had changed colour and was now white, like mayonnaise.

Suddenly Auntie Mona's car came up the drive. At first Uncle Vern did not hear. The Doctor gathered his things quickly.

Uncle Vern, hearing Auntie Mona's footsteps outside, dived for the couch. He was snoring when he hit it and would not be contactable for the next six hours at least.

Auntie Mona came in the back door as the Doctor was leaving.

"See ya later, Mona, "he said as he passed her in the hall. Her only response was to jump into the air with a surprised look on her face.

Polo lay in a snoring heap on the floor. There was broken glass everywhere and the room reeked of beer and cigarettes. She had not yet noticed the guinea pig in the microwave, or the goat's skull of urine on the mantlepiece, or the table things in the linen press. Uncle Vern was snoring loudly.

"I see Uncle Vern has been getting in touch with the dark side, "she said without anger or surprise." God I'm tired from dancing! I could use a pick-me-up... "

Then she noticed the bottle of rollmops on the sideboard.

"Mmm, rollmops, "she said.

I should have spoken but was so stunned that I did not get the chance to warn her.

She picked up the bottle and glanced around at the wreckage." I am a feeling a little peckish, "she said." That's funny I meant to get the ones in brine, but I must have picked up the mayonnaise ones by mistake, "she added, picking one out with her fingers and putting it in her mouth.

That was all she said. She began chewing the rollmop, then an awful look of recognition crawled across her face like a spider and she dropped the jar and ran from the room.

The bathroom door slammed.

The retching noises continued for some time so I decided that just for once I could go to bed without doing my teeth. In the morning, I thought, as I lay in bed listening to the lonely sounds of Auntie Mona ruining her best dress, I would get up really early, before anyone else, and go for a long walk.

FEAR OF FLYING

a legend of the blue Vern

And Uncle Vern Story: Do Not Induce Vomiting

The time to go had been and gone and still my parents hadn't come. I couldn't understand it. It was not as if there were not regular air services to Fiji. They could have phoned. It was not unusual that the phone hadn't rung for several days. I was sitting in the kitchen, bored stiff, wondering what to do, when I noticed that the phone cord had been unplugged in such a way that it was hardly noticeable. I felt - I feared - I knew that this was Uncle Vern's work. Uncle Vern would miss me fearfully when I left. His attempts to bond with me had taken on greater urgency over the previous two days. Only hours before, at four in the morning, he had almost forced open my bedroom door in an attempt to show me his train set.

I plugged in the phone. It rang. I answered it.

"Uncle Vern and Auntie Mona's farm, "I said," Reginald speaking. "

"Reginald! Thank God it's you! "said my mother." We'll be there in twenty five minutes! "she added and then she hung up. It was great to hear Mum's voice again.

I had to get to the gate without being seen. I felt bad about not thanking Auntie Mona for all she had done for me, the cooking and the washing and all that stuff, but she was down at Polo's having a cappuccino.

Uncle Vern was down behind the toolshed caponizing the young roosters. I knew how engrossed he could get in that work and I prayed that he would be at it for a while.

Just like Chuck Norris in ' Rotors Over Rotorua' I kept my head down and dashed along the privet hedge and tumbled over the bank by the corral and onto the drive. So far so good. As I walked down the drive, looking anxiously back at the toolshed, Uncle Vern came out from behind a gum tree and grabbed me by the shoulder. I jumped a foot and felt ever so guilty.

"Reginald! "he said.

"Uncle Vern! "I said.

"Reg! Your heart's beating so fast! "said Uncle Vern.

He touched me on the chest with the palm of his hand. It was an unusually close incursion into my personal space. His hand was rough and hot and sticky . I froze.

                    And Uncle Vern Story: Do Not Induce Vomiting

"Reg, "he said sympathetically," you're missing your Mum and Dad, aren't you! They'll be here soon, son. I'm sure they will. There, there: they're bound to call soon. "

He grasped my shoulders. My upper body was pulled forward but my feet edged away. He hugged me to himself awkwardly. He was breathing heavily. The stench of the beer and rollmops he had had for lunch was revolting.

"There, there! "he said.

I vomitted on him slightly. I couldn't help it.

"It's nothing, Reg, nothing, "he said, wiping it into the fabric with his hand." Auntie Mona will get it out in the wash, it's nothing. I don't mind it at all, really, Reg. Don't be ashamed, son. There should be no shame between us, Reg. We are as shameless as newborn babes. "

It was horrible. He let me go. Then he took my hand for a moment and then let it go and then he burst into song.

"Bird gotta swim, fish gotta fly

Man just gotta sit and wonder

Why? Why? Why? "

Then he said," Come, come. Walk with me. You'll see the things I see. "

I hesitated.

"Don't think twice, son, it's all right. "

I thought it best to give the lead so I began to walk towards the gate. Uncle Vern walked alongside me and said,

"Have you ever wondered why men can't fly, Reg "

"No, Uncle Vern, "I said.

"Haven't you? "

"No. "

"Oh. "

"Sorry, Uncle Vern. "

"That's ok, Reg. Why are we walking so fast? Slow down and I'll tell you a small story. "

I didn't feel up to it and couldn't help groaning.

"No, I promise, Reg, this one's minute. There was a young bull and an old bull on a hillside overlooking a paddock full of cows. The young bull said to the old bull ' Let's run down there and say hello to a few of those cows.' The old bull said to the young bull, "No, let's walk down there and say hello to all of them.'"

        And Uncle Vern Story: Do Not Induce Vomiting

He laughed heartily. I did not see the joke.

"Get it," he said. "Say hello to 'em! Ha! Ha!"

Uncle Vern laughed and I did the best I could. Then Uncle Vern fell silent as if he were at a loss for words. Something was exercising him. He began to hum an old song.

"Would you like to fly in my beautiful balloon...up, up and away in my beautiful balloon...fly me to the moon and let me play among the stars...Uranus is much bigger than Mars...down, down, down I go, round, round, round I go, in a spin, lovin' that spin I'm in..."

He broke off his medley and grasped me by the shoulders again and looked deeply, searchingly into my eyes. I noticed that his cataracts would need another operation soon.

"Men can fly, Reg. That's what I want to tell you, son, men can fly. Do you want me to tell you about it, to show you what I mean?

My parents were due in about twelve minutes. There could be no harm.

"Sure, Uncle Vern, "I said.

We sat down on the bank by the moat. As I gazed fixedly into the muddy creek that struggled along down there he made an extraordinary claim.

"I know that of which I speak, Reg. I know a man can fly because I have flown myself. "

"In an aeroplane, Uncle Vern? "I said, impressed, because in those days few people from that district had flown in aeroplanes.

"No, Reg! Don't be ridiculous! Those things are unsafe and you will never get me up in one of them. I have flown unaided. Like a bird. The Aborigines had wise men who were said to be able to fly and I have done it myself and can vouch for the truth of it."

He paused so that I could catch up with the full import of what he had said.

"Gee, Uncle Vern, that's amazing! "

"Would you like to know how to fly, Reg? "

"No, not really, Uncle Vern "I said.

"No? What sort of boy are you, Reg? Surely the exhilaration of flying through the air free like a bird must have some appeal to any boy who has breath in his lungs? "

"I am afraid of heights, Uncle Vern, "I said feebly.

"Do not be afraid, Reg. Heights are not the problem, believe me, I was afraid of heights myself, but do you know what a fear of heights really is? It is a fear of edges. It is a fear of being on the threshold. It is a fear

                And Uncle Vern Story: Do Not Induce Vomiting

of change, of transition and of plunging a hundred feet to your death.It is a fear of losing control. But in flying there are no edges, you do not lose control you are in control and instead of destroying you, flying gives you unbridled power, Reg, unbridled power. Now what do you say to that? "

"Gee, since you put it that way, Uncle Vern... "I offered.

"I was about your age, Reg, a little older perhaps, a gangly youth with no idea of anything in the world when I first discovered how to fly. At first it was just a dream, a dream so vivid that for a while after waking up I thought that I had actually been flying. I had been dreaming that I was down at the dam swimming. I dove in but as I sailed over the water I did not go down into it but skimmed over the surface and landed on my feet on the other side. I was amazed so I dove again. The same thing happened. I felt a sort of power as the water seemed to repel me. Each time I did it I felt the power within me and then on one dive I thought, 'Go for it Vern!' and I went for it. I believed I could fly and I could fly and I did fly. I skimmed just over the top of the long grass. It was the most amazing experience of my life. I flew a hundred yards, straight into a big pile of hay. I hadn't discovered how to stop or steer at that stage. My cousin Wendy was in the haystack at the time and boy! did she get a surprise! The next night I went flying again....

"From then on every night I went flying. I got better and better at it. I always had to take off over water, for some reason. At first it was mostly over the dam but later on I took off over ponds, lakes, rivers and streams, municipal swimming pools, the ocean, any kind of water at all. I dived from buildings and from trees. I tried smaller and smaller bodies of water: creeks, puddles, glasses, leaky radiators and beads of dew gathered in the cleavages of blades of grass.

"At first I was always afraid when I took off, especially when I leapt from tall places like treetops but after a while I got my confidence. "

"And this was all in dreams, Uncle Vern? "

"Well, no, son, that was just the point. If it was just dreams it would mean nothing, would it? No, son, dreaming is just garbage, and you would be far better off if you paid your dreams no more attention than you pay the racket the garbage men make outside your bedroom window once a week in town!

"But the dreams were useful as practice. One night, a full moon night, I got up real quiet like and snuck out of the house and went down to the dam in my pyjamas. I knew I could do it and I could do it and I did do it. I took a real long run at it and I dove and skimmed across the dam and guess what? Yep, I took off. I do not mind telling you, Reg, I was surprised at my own power, and at first I was real scared. I mean before I knew it I was up high, really high, and flying fast.

"It was a bit awkward too, because you know what flies on pyjamas are like! Just imagine if one of them old biddies in Wallabong had gone outside for a call of nature or something and looked up and saw me flying in the moonlight in my glory! There were all kinds of difficulties and dangers that I hadn't considered. Nevertheless, when you're on a good thing, stick to it! And I did.

"Flying is fantastic, Reg. I learnt to climb and dive, to speed up and slow down, to hover, to do loop-the-loop and barrel rolls I flew up over the high country and saw young brumby stallions fighting on rocky crag and I skimmed along mountain streams watching young platypuses at play. I flew over Bairnsdale and believe you me Reg, you can see some wonderful things in Bairnsdale late at night, women who have difficulty sleeping and suchlike disporting themselves in the backyards, the activity in lovers' lane and all the rest of it. I flew over Sale but I had to leave Sale because they sent a couple of Vampire jets up after me thinking that I was a UFO. Those old Vampires were no match for me, though, no sir! I went down to a level where they couldn't follow or get me on their radar. I must have been doing a hundred miles an hour only inches from the ground. By that time I knew what I was doing. Mind you, this was still my first flight, you know. The only problem I had was that I didn't know how to land.

"Instinct told me to try the dam at home. Just before dawn I came in for the final approach. The birds were just beginning to wake up, and they were making a big racket on account of me being in their airspace. My attention was distracted for a moment near the windbreak and I clipped a tree and began spinning out of control but as I fell over the edge of the dam I managed to pull out of the dive and crash landed on the edge of the dam.

"They found me there in the morning covered in grazes and dew and frogspawn and dead asleep. The doc said I had been somnambulistic, so they tied me down to the bed for the next two weeks. I couldn't fly. It was terrible, Reg, terrible, being young and fit and not allowed to fly. Not that I told them I could fly. No way. As soon as they untied me, though, I went out again. I mean, Reg, what could a poor boy do? I had to.

"Magnificent was the only word for it. I could see everything, and I could go everywhere. But I only flew at night. Something told me, some deep instinct warned me to keep it a secret. Nevertheless when I wasn't near home, I mean, in this district - I used to cover a lot of ground, Reg, even just in one night - I made sure I put on a good show.

"People were awestruck. I would swoop down and do amazing things and then fly away again and they were left wondering if it really happened or if it was just a trick of the wind. I flew over deserts and forests amd cities and beaches and the sea. I was super, Reg, super!

"The power I had was immeasurable, but there was a price. It was very dangerous and even frightening at times. Sometimes I crashed into trees and then my fear of heights would play merry hell with me as I tried to climb down. I fell through city canyons and was only saved by the awnings of swish hotels and then I had to escape crowds of curious onlookers. And I couldn't land safely except over water, just like taking off. So, in the morning when I got up my pyjamas would be wet and my mother would want to know the reason why...I mean I couldn't tell them I'd been flying, could I? No. It really taxed me to think up excuses four or five mornings a week and from time to time they would tie me down at night time when I was found sleeping in the paddocks. I even got accused of being a chronic bedwetter. But they never broke my spirit or my desire to fly, Reg, never! "

This was even more far-fetched than usual, and yet there was a powerful compulsion in the way he told it that almost carried me along with its conviction.

"Do you still go flying, Uncle Vern? "I asked.

"Only very occasionally, Reg, very occasionally now. It's a game for the young and the fit. You could do it, Reg, easily, especially with me here to help you with some pointers. The main thing, Reg, the key thing, is that you have to believe. You've gotta have faith. That is paramount. If you believe and you have strong faith and desire to be the best you can be, and you've got an experienced friend to help you fly, why, then, Reg, the sky is the only limit! "

Uncle Vern's hand had been resting on my shoulder for some time. He began to knead my earlobe with his fingers. I reached for my pocket knife just in case.

"Do you want to fly, Reg? Would you like to soar like a God? Would you like me to show you how to do it? It would be the greatest gift I could bestow upon you, son, and all you would have to do is believe that you can do it and have faith in me. Trust me, Reg. Believe in us and mankind, take my hand and fly with me! Even this pathetic little creek down here would be enough to make us soar, Reg! Have faith! "

Uncle Vern indicated the muddy rivulet in the ditch below us. We were doomed, of course. How could I believe? I was more mindful of Uncle Vern's enthusiastic viewing of the mud wrestling at the hotel last week. I did not jump when he did but I went into the moat anyway because he grabbed my wrist and pulled me in.

What happened next was one of the most disgusting things that had ever happened to me. There was something in the mud. I mean apart from the slippery rocks on the bottom that made standing impossible. Perhaps they were eels, mud eels, as Uncle Vern said. They squirmed all over us, trying to gain access to every clothing orifice, trousers legs, sleeves, necks, everywhere. For a minute at least Uncle Vern and I struggled to gain our feet, alternately supporting each other and falling together. Uncle Vern was laughing strangely. I felt myself becoming seriously unbuttoned in every sense when the Merc suddenly appeared at the gate just above us, the horn tooted, and then my mother looked down and saw us. I scrambled up the bank. Uncle Vern, realizing belatedly that my parents had arrived, clambered up after me, his gleaming false teeth grinning foolishly through the mud.

Mother was aghast.

"What have you been doing, Reginald? "

She was so stunned that she did not have time to lock the doors. I got in the back.

"Laocoon! "I said, knowing she would be impressed with something cultural." The Daytrap players are going to perform a frieze of Laocoon and Uncle Vern is in the leading role. We have been rehearsing. "

"Where are your things? Oh, never mind, we can get some more. Hurry Alphonse! "

"Good Lord! "declared my father," that mud stinks! "

"Quick, "cried Mother," here he comes, drive, damn you! "

"We should at least say hello, "said my father.

Uncle Vern approached the driver's side. He almost leant on it but then, appreciating the polished cream duco, held back.

"Hi Alphonse! "he said with genuine friendliness." How's it goin'? "

"Good Merv! How are you? "

I wished, despite everything, I wished that just once they could get his name right.

"Can't complain. Who'd listen? Wouldja like to come in for a cuppa? "

"I'd love to, Merv.. "began my father, but my mother, bless her, leaned across him and said,

"Merv, darling, I'm sorry, but we have to get Reg back on the bus for boarding school in Melbourne tonight at eight so we have to get a move on, I'm afraid. Next time, darling, hmmmn? "

She held a hatpin close to my father and whispered fiercely to him," Drive fast now or you get it. "

With no further ado my father sped off, leaving Uncle Vern in a shower of dust and gravel. I looked back at him. He waved us goodbye. I waved back. He kept waving for a long time. It was pathetic. If it hadn't been for everything I might almost have felt sorry for him. My father said,

"Magda, we really should stop one day and at least have a cup of coffee with them. "

"Alphonse, you are an imbecile, "said my mother." That man is no better than an animal. "

"Really, Magda, that's hardly fair. Admittedly I don't know him, but I must say that Merv doesn't seem a bad fellow. "

"Forget it! "she said with finality.

Then my mother said," Stop the car! "

My father stopped.

"Reg, get out. The smell is too much. Get the rag from the boot and wipe that seat and then get in the boot. Hurry! "

I did so. She sprayed the car with an upmarket toilet freshener. I got into the boot and pulled it closed. It was good to be home again. The smell of the fumes was very strong and I was soon asleep. I dreamt I was back at the 'Breakaways'. I was walking down to the toolshed. It was sunset. The dream was in vivid colour, I always dream in colour. It was one of those days when it rains on one side of the road but not the other - that often happens in the Daytrap district.

Everything was unnaturally silent. The peacock barked noiselessly at me from its perch in the tamarillo tree. My footsteps made no sound. The spring shower falling heavily on the tin roof made no sound. There was no wall at the far south side of the toolshed where the tractor was parked. Uncle Vern, a stubby in his right hand, a corncob in his left, his shirt-tail hanging out, his trousers hanging low, stood there gazing out at the great, gaunt stag on the river flat. The sun, setting as if over the whole world, and not just over Daytrap, cast ethereal hues on its ghostly grey trunk.

Uncle Vern turned towards me without moving as if he were mounted on a lazy Susan. Big, fat tears were streaming down his face. It was an unnerving sight and I wondered what dreadful thing had happened to produce this effect in him. He spoke to me. I could not hear his words but I could read his lips. Pointing to the tin roof with the forefinger of his corncob hand, with an air of blessedness, just like Leonardo's picture of St John, he said,

"Listen to that! That's the most beautiful sound in Australia. "

That's all he said, and he just stood there, crying like a baby.

THE JACARANDA TREE

a tale of uncertainty

An Auntie Mona Story: Whispering is rude

It was raining. Auntie Mona was at the sink peeling potatoes under a running tap. I was sitting at the kitchen table working on my 'Sunball' competition entry. Uncle Vern was still in hospital and would not be home for another day. He had spent three whole days in the isolation ward at the Bairnsdale hospital. Later we heard that this had been a busy time for Uncle Vern and the hospital, but life at the farm was very quiet, as quiet, as Uncle Vern would have said, as female wind.

It had been a funny morning. The day had begun in brilliant sunshine but then the wind sprang up and a big front came over the hills and everything went still. There was a flash of lightning and a thunderclap. An inch of rain fell in five minutes and stopped as if it had never happened and sunlight poured into the house again. Double rainbows appeared in the sky, straddling the river just upstream of Daytrap. Through the kitchen window, looking up the valley, we could see them as clear as anything. The high wind pushed the clouds about like so much stage furniture and we had another sunny spell. Then it began to rain again.

Everything was still except the rain. Auntie Mona stopped peeling the potatoes and hung her arms limply in the sink as she gazed out the windows. It was not raining heavily but because the spouting was slightly broken water poured over the kitchen window as if it were being hosed down. I did not know what she was looking at because I could see only the back of her head.

She rinsed the red loam from the spuds and put them, two at a time, into her dented steel colander. Then she filled the sink with hot water and detergent and began to wash the dishes.

When Auntie Mona finished washing the dishes she continued to stand at the sink and waited patiently for the grey water to drain, scraping the humble detritus of our breakfast from the sink strainer with her cracked, pink dishwater fingers. She fell silent for a time as she concentrated on this task and then she sighed, the sort of sigh you'd bet she wasn't even aware of, just like when Uncle Vern swore softly when he put his boots on each morning.

The rain stopped. Sunlight filled the kitchen again. Still Auntie Mona did not move. She was standing on her left leg, and her right leg was tucked behind the left and rested on its own toes. I knew she was thinking because for the first time in ages she had stopped talking.

Just as Uncle Vern, by the years of his prime, had accumulated certain medical conditions, so had Auntie Mona fallen victim to Prolixia Nervosa, a disease which, while not deadly like, say, cervical cancer, was nevertheless capable of blighting the life of its sufferers and their families and friends. Although rarely mentioned, especially in womens' magazines, it was in fact the second commonest disease in Australia, after dandruff, and it was the indirect cause of countless other social ills. This cruel disease afflicted women of a certain age, cutting across all barriers of class, and creed, although, according to Uncle Vern who had told me about it, it was extremely rare among the lower races.

I remember when Auntie Mona first married Uncle Vern. She had not exactly been the blushing bride - she wore pink - though she still retained her engaging, youthfully-feminine, speech habit of turning the ends of her sentences up? You know what I mean? So that everything she said sounded submissive and hopeful? Like a question? But since then the pressure of married life had rendered her speech as flat and nasal as a banana pancake.

And she talked nearly all the time. It was as if her inner voice had escaped from its iron lung and suffered brain damage. I had long ago learned not to pay much attention to what Auntie Mona said.

Suddenly something happened that happened every now and then. Keeping glass clean was more than a duty for Auntie Mona, it was a religion, so birds often came to grief by crashing into the farmhouse windows.

A grey shrike-thrush which had been singing in the birdbath by the kitchen, perhaps mistaking Auntie Mona for a tree, flew into the window, broke its neck and fell dead to the ground. At this Auntie Mona burst into a fit of uncontrollable laughter, and then she began to sob piteously.

I didn't know what to do. Obviously she needed comforting. I went and stood behind her.

"Auntie Mona... "I said.

She sobbed louder.

Apart from the usual kisses on the cheek I had very little physical contact with Auntie Mona. Nevertheless, desperate measures were required, so I grasped her shoulders gently and said,

"Auntie Mona, please! Come and sit down. I'll make you a nice cup of tea. "

She allowed herself to be led to the kitchen table and sat down and I made her a nice hot pot of her favorite blend, Ty-Nee-Tips. Uncle Vern preferred Amgoorie. My own favorite was Payless, but that is neither here nor there.

While I was at the stove she went to the glass cabinet and got out her photo albums. Albums. It's funny, but when I saw her fondly turning the pages I thought of Uncle Vern and the way he said 'albums', making it sound like a man's name. There was no doubt about it, it had to be admitted: despite everything, we missed Uncle Vern. His absence did not make our lives seem empty, exactly, but they were certainly less eventful. I wasn't sure what Auntie Mona was looking for in the albums.

It definitely was not pictures of Uncle Vern, of which there were very few because he had always been camera shy ever since his shocking experiences as an undercover man in the sexual revolution.

No, she was looking at the old photos, the ones of her and her family when she was a young girl, growing up on the farm near Lucknow, outside of Bairnsdale. While she was engrossed in her pictures I arranged a pretty plate of iced vovos and brought her her cup of tea.

"Thank-you Reg, "she said." I don't care what anyone says, you're a good boy. I'm sorry Reg, forgive me for being like this. Oh, God, I feel such a fool. I don't know why I'm like this, unless... "

Her voice trailed off.

"Unless what, Auntie Mona? "

"Nothing, Reg, it's nothing, "she said." Ah, Reg, look at these pictures. Just look. It was a different world then. You know Reg, I know I am the same person, and yet I feel so different now. I wouldn't say I was happy then, but I was hopeful. Do you know what I mean Reg? No, you can't, you couldn't possibly. "

She shook her head.

"Maybe I do Auntie Mona, "I said." The other day, you may think this is silly, but last week I started to feel that I wanted to be a ringtail possum. "

I must have said this with some force of conviction for she turned and looked at me as if I had actually said something.

"It's not easy for you is it Reg, "she said." I know how it is. Look at those date palms, "she said, suddenly changing the subject and drawing my attention to a photo of the old homestead.

"Norwood. Ah, Norwood. Look at those date palms! And that beautiful lawn! Norwood was the biggest house on the biggest property in the district. Sheep and dairy cattle. If anyone went to Lucknow looking for work as likely as not the townsfolk would tell them to try Norwood, and if there was anything at all that might pass for employment then they would have it, at least a day's work. A 'darg', that's what Father used to call it. "I can give ye but a darg, friend," he would say, "but I can give ye that at least. There he is, on the verandah, with Mother."

The photo showed a stern-looking man seated in a large cane armchair and gazing firmly over the photographer's shoulder. Behind him, to his right, stood a solid, ruddy-looking woman in a clean apron, resting a hand on his shoulder and staring proudly, even defiantly at the camera. A dog lazed uninterestedly at their feet. Stone columns holding up the verandah and tall windows dark in shade conveyed the substance and stolidity of a well-to-do rural family of that era. The image was saved from a stiff, headstone formality only by the fact that Auntie Mona's 'mother' had severely crossed eyes. I succeeded in not laughing at the picture.

Auntie Mona eased the corners of the photo out of the page and held it closer to me.

"You can see one of the rose bushes," she said. "They had the most beautiful drive lined with magnificent roses and in summer just being near them was like being in a perfume shop. Father used to sit on the verandah and watch people walk up the drive. It was a long walk. He used to watch the way they walked. He used to say that every man had his own walk and that you could read their walks the same way you could read their handwriting. That's what he said.

"My half-sister, Ruth, and I used to watch them too, from our room upstairs, or from the path at the side of the house. We used to watch for the way they wore their hats. Everyone wore hats in those days. A man with his brim down in the front had something to hide. A man with a horizontal brim was religious. A man with his hat high on his forehead was innocent. A hat on an angle indicated a degree of devilishness. We learnt that from reading Lord Baden-Powell's book, "Scouting for Boys" . We always wanted to join the Guides but there were no Guides in our district so we never did.

"Father knew those men well. As they came up the drive he would say 'single' or 'married'. And if it was married he would say 'six months' or 'a year' or 'five years' or 'ten years', meaning that was how long it had been since the man had seen his family. He reckoned that the best workers were the ones that had been away from their families the longest because they had their minds on the job. Nevertheless he used to try to persuade some of them to go back to their homes, the ones that had been on the road since the early thirties. After they had been there a while he used to invite them into the smoking room. Ruth and I sometimes listened at the door or the window. He would give them a cigar and tell them how much he liked them and then offer them their fare and some spending money if they would go home. Not once did a man take the money.

"I can't go back now! "they'd say." It's been too long. The kids wouldn't remember me. I can't remember the youngest one's name. They're better off without me. Besides, there'll be someone else by now. "

Sometimes they'd even cry. Father could be a cruel man, I realize that now. I used to feel so sorry for those men. Ruth would laugh at them, but then she was older than me. Father would sit there in his squeaking chair, rocking back and forth on it while they composed themselves and left in silence. That was his way of sacking them."

She turned the photo over.

"There's writing on the back!" she said. "What does it say, Reg? I haven't got my glasses."

I read it and told her,

"It says, 'I told her not to look straight at the camera. This picture is completely ruined.'"

"Oh. That's Father, of course!" she said quietly as she replaced the picture and turned the page.

"Mother and Father were not really my actual parents. They were my Uncle and Aunt by marriage, I think. I know I was not theirs, but they never really spoke about it."

The pictures on the next page were all of a family picnic in the bush.

"This was at The Falls on Boxing Day. There's Mother and Father. Me. I can't hardly have been more than six. Ruth. Grandma Olsen. The Dochertys. There's Peter Abbott and his sister, Rebecca. At school they used to call them Peter and Rebecca Rabbit. They both died during the war. He was in a prison camp, and she died of complications. See the truck, that must have been in the middle of the Depression with all those hungry boards set up. Nowadays you call them greedy boards. That's our dog, Phillip. He lived to be twenty-nine years old! It was such simple fare, but they were days of luxury for us..."

The women were mostly smiling in this picture, and so were some of the men. She turned the page again. This time it was shearing time, and the pictures were full of the workers in their sheds, at the holding pens or hard at it in the shearing shed. There was a picture of little Auntie Mona lying in a half-full wool bale. And of her father standing in an authoritative pose and the men standing around laughing.

"I loved it when the men came. They used to spoil us something shocking," said Auntie Mona. "I suppose a lot of them missed their own children. They used to play with us and tell us stories. Dog stories. The ways of catching rabbits. Snake facts. Do you know, Reg, that a snake never dies until sundown? And if you kill a snake its mate will come looking for you? And snakes never open their eyes! That's true!"

The hall clock chimed, as it did every quarter hour. It was a musty old sound which I did not like at all.

"That clock was Mother's," said Auntie Mona, as she turned another page.

This was full of photo's of the garden, as was the next page and the one after. Auntie Mona featured in several photos and one could see that even when she was young she had been very ordinary looking. She looked at them closely, and went back and forth through the album as if searching for something. The garden was a typical old style country garden. Loveliness without elegance. Relaxed. A casual, lived-in beauty. The front garden was divided into two halves by the rose-lined, gravel drive. In the centre of each half there was a circular garden bed surrounded by lawn, Two palm trees stood at the gate like sentinels. The back garden had the inevitable lemon tree and some plums or nectarines growing out of the lawn, a magnolia tree, a daisy bush, and asters. It rambled on past the garage and some outhouses to a vegetable patch and beyond that, the paddocks, and beyond them, the mountains and the sky.

"That's funny!" said Auntie Mona.

"What, Auntie Mona?" I asked.

"The jacaranda tree," said my Aunt, "there used to be the most beautful jacaranda tree in the backyard. Mother and Father planted it there when they first moved into the house. I remember it so well. It was like a purple waterfall in summer and such a lovely shade to sit under! Have a look, Reg, can you see a jacaranda tree? Maybe these were taken after that unfortunate accident. There was a sad story, Reg."

I could see no jacaranda tree, nor any sign of a stump.

"Would you like another cup of tea, Auntie Mona?" I asked.

"Yes, why, thank-you, Reg," she said, "that would be nice. Is the pot still warm? Don't bother making a new one if it's still warm."

"I'll just top it up with some hot water," I said

As I waited for the jug to boil again, Auntie Mona began to tell her story.

"When I was about fourteen years old, Reg, maybe a bit older, about your age, I suppose, I particularly remember one young man who came up our drive. He was younger than most of them in fact he was not much older than I was, I suppose. Now that I think back on it, he can't have been.

"As he came up the drive we couldn't help noticing his jaunty walk, though he was somewhat bowlegged. His hat was on an angle. We always looked out for that. He sported a red bandana. Also, there was a sock hanging out the bottom of his bedroll. Isn't it funny what can stick in your mind for nearly forty years!

"His name was Max and he was a German refugee. He walked up the drive, whistling gaily, and when he reached the verandah where Father was he said ' Howdy! ' just like a German cowboy. His English wasn't very good, nevertheless Father employed him. Everyone got a chance.

"Max was a willing worker but he was also accident prone. The was always a funny story about Max. He was good humoured about it. "Vell, I zuppoze zey must find it ferry funny!" he would say. At night-time he would sit outside his hut after work and play a little squeezebox. It was so charming, Reg, to be out there in the bush and hear the lovely foreign serenade.

"I can still remember those German songs, 'Edelweiss' and 'O Tannenbaum'. They were the only two he knew. And after a week or so Father took to putting beeswax in his ears of an evening. But I never tired of the music and I would often listen from a distance.

"One night he called me over.

"'Mona. Come, Mona, und zit by me, if you wish!'

"Well, of course, I did.

"'Hello, Max! ' I said.

"' Hello, Mona, mein liebling.' he said.

"He always called me that.

"' You look ferry pretty in zat blue dress, Mona. All day I huff bin sinking zis, you know.' "

"I blushed. ' Gosh, Max!' I said. ' Father will be after you with a gun!'

"' Where?' said Max. He was really alarmed.

"' I'm only joking, Max! ' I said.

"'Please, Mona, liebling, I come from Deutschland, ja!'

"I did not know what he meant.

"' You..you cannot understand, 'he said.

"' Understand what, Max?'

"' Nussing. Das is nussing, Mona. Vood you like for me to tell you a story, hmm? Ein little story, liebling? '

"' Sure, Max!' I said.

"' Ven I vos in Chermany I was a student, ja. I vos studying to be a stationmaster for zer trains. Und zair vos anozzer student, she vos mein special friend, ja. Her name vos Heidi She had zer schwartz, is ah, black, ja? ja, zer black hair und she vos ferry pretty. In zer efenings ve vood vork along zer riffer, arm in arm mit all zer uzzer junge couples. In zer summer ve ver to be merried. In April, two years ago, zer vedding vos meant to be. In April 1935 But it could not be. Nien."

"' What happened to her Max? ' I said.

"' Nien, nien,' he said.

"' Did she get hit by a train, Max? ' I asked because I had no idea

"' Nien liebling, nicht train,' said Max.

"There were tears running down his face, Reg, it was awful!

"I touched his shoulder, Reg, I touched his shoulder and said, 'Don't worry, Max, it can't be that bad.' but that only made him cry more.

"' What was it, Max? ' I asked, because I just didn't understand. I didn't understand anything, Reg. They never told us anything.

"' Max was crying on my shoulder, Reg, but I was just a girl. I stroked his hair

"' What was it Max? ' I asked and I gave him my hanky.

"He blew his nose. And then he looked at me and then he looked away across the fields. ' She vos a chew,' he said.

"I thought about this for a minute and then I asked him, 'What's a chew, Max?'

"He gave me the strangest puzzled look, Reg, and then he said,

"' You know, liebling, I don't know. I don't know myself.'

"And he half laughed and half cried and hugged me and said how much he loved this country. Then I had to go inside because mother was calling for me.

"The next morning was a Saturday and Mother and Father had gone out to Lucknow in the trap. Max was up and about early, fixing things and cleaning things, he was ever so busy. When he saw me he gave me a big kiss on the cheek, like a brother might have done Reg, that's all, and he wished me good morning and said that he loved this country so much and my father was the best of men and he was going to work hard all day for my father. I had never seen him so happy.

"But it was not to last, Reg. Later that morning he did something he should never have done. It was not his fault because in Germany they did not have Jacaranda trees so how was he to know that the Jacaranda tree was not dead. That's what he thought, and he got the axe and chopped it down. When Father and Mother saw what he had done they were horrified. The symbol of their love, and their marriage and all they had built was destroyed.

Father went straight down to his shack. When Max saw Father he smiled broadly thinking that Father had come to thank him for all the extra work he had done on his afternoon off but instead of that Father was in such a rage that all he could do was to roar at poor Max,

"GET OUT OF MY PLACE!"

"He threw a pound at him, two ten shilling notes, and pointed to the gate.

"Max did not understand, but he could see - anyone could see - that Father could not be reasoned with. I was so embarrassed. I followed Max down the drive, but my father called out to me to stop. So I ran behind the house, I was crying Reg, really crying. You've no idea how awful it was. Just when you got to make friends with the men, they would be gone. I ran around behind the milking sheds and through the windbreak and called to Max who was on the road. He came to me. He was crying too, Reg. He said to me,

"'Don't cry, mein liebling,' but neither of us could help it.

"In the end he had to go, to find a place to camp for the night. I wished I could have gone with him, but he gave me a hug and he said, 'People always hate refugees, liebling, especially refugees from love.' Isn't that beautiful, Reg. For three days after that I didn't eat a thing, Reg, from sheer shame and anger at how they had treated that poor young man. No matter how much they loved their jacaranda tree, it was wrong.

"And you know what, Reg? That tree didn't die at all. It grew back the next year with three trunks and it had far more flowers than it had ever had before and was much more beautiful and much better than it had been. Much. Oh, Reg, times have changed so much. I feel quite old just thinking about it. No one finds corn pads in the alabaster cuspidor in the vestibule any more. And I guess I'm not unhappy about that...father was so..."

The phone rang.

"Auntie Mona and Uncle Vern's farm," I said, "Reginald speaking."

It was the hospital for Auntie Mona. She listened for a time and then said quietly,

"Oh, I see," and replaced the receiver on its cradle.

"What is it Auntie Mona?" I asked.

"It's your Uncle," she said. "He's better. They're sending him home early. He'll be home tomorrow."

"That's good," I said.

"Yeah, great," she said, without enthusiasm. The she packed away the albums and blew her nose. Her attack of weepiness was over. The strong, Australian, afternoon sun shone through the house. As I heard the distant sound of Auntie Mona talking to herself while she went about her household chores, I wondered whether I was glad things were back to normal, or not.

AFTERWORD

When the Court declared Reginald R. Wells dead the family's attention was drawn by his executors to certain chattels held at a self-storage facility in Nowra, N.S.W. Most of these effects (cheap furniture, old musical instruments and assorted bric-a-brac,) were surrendered to cover his outstanding debt.

All that remained was a tin trunk containing a motley collection of curios and a mass of papers, including a diary of exhorbitant length. It was from these documents that the following volume was culled.

The reader will soon realize that Reginald's literary skills were at best rudimentary. Nevertheless he has managed to convey, with an unconscious poignancy, the struggle of a young person to come to terms with an environment that he found threatening, though by no means hostile.

This modest book was produced first and foremost as a family memento. The print run has been extended slightly to allow the general public to help defray the printing costs. To that end some illustrations have been provided by a journeyman artist (R.Moss) and packed in vacuum sealed plastic with the usual warnings. These embellishments should be understood simply as gimmicks designed to secure a niche market and in no way reflecting the values, thoughts or feelings of Reginald or the family. Indeed there are no dirty words in the book as Reginald never used bad language himself, especially in front of women. It was his upbringing.

I should point out that the stories have largely been imposed upon the manuscript. There was no semblance of organisation in Reginald's work and I might add that the effort involved in deciphering his childish handwriting and execrable spelling was not inconsiderable.

Naturally all names in this book have been changed, including Reginald's. The possible sources of the material have strenuously denied all knowledge of the contents. As honest, upright, country folk they are to be believed. One can only assume that Reginald, always a solitary boy, sought in these fictions an imaginative escape from a rural life into which he never seemed to fit.

It remains only to acknowledge the generous (unpaid) assistance of certain individuals who helped see the work into print. The typing was done by Claude Rossi. Brother Cobbett of the Terminal Institute gave freely of his time and advice. Phil Edwards was poof reader. Monsignor Desmond Bockholt's spiritual guidance was indispensable throughout the project. My sincere thanks to all.

P.S. There never was a Jacaranda tree at the property supposedly in question in the eponymous story. Magda and Alphonse D'Oyly-Wells were tragically killed in a plane crash in Ecuador in 1989. They are survived by a number of frozen foetuses.

REGINALD: A MEMOIR

I cannot say that I knew Reginald well, but then no one did.

The circumstances of his birth are unusually obscure considering that we live in the Age of Information. Family tradition has it that he was left as a foundling at the door of a Christian Brothers' establishment as a temporary measure and that he was reclaimed following a brief court case. However there are no records to support this.

Certainly his parents were very busy people. They traveled extensively and Reginald largely grew up at St Gary's boarding school and at a farm in the country where he spent his holidays.

It was at boarding school where we met. I was the French master. Reginald was five. Though we were related we did not talk much as we moved in very different circles. We were never intimate. Even at that early time it quickly became apparent that Reginald was a loner, an outsider and at times, it must be said, a pariah dog.

He did not have a good time at school. Though adequate at his classes he seemed unable to agree with anyone. To his credit he did eventually learn to shut up and be sneaky.

While he thoroughly disliked school he always seemed oddly pleased to return each term. His holidays seemed to take something from him, and to take him further from normal people. Physically his condition improved when he was away from school, but when he came back there was something about his eyes, a harrowed and harrowing look that made people turn away. But little heed was paid to this as there were many other boys whose holidays affected them similarly so it was nothing unusual.

Of his interests there is little to be said. He collected bugs and beetles and the like. He maintained many cases of them and curiously he was known to mount live insects. They would squirm on their pins for days, weeks even, until they died. Naturally they were hardly what you'd call fine specimens by then, especially the soft-bodied ones. This hobby was drawn to the attention of the Senior Master who on questioning the lad was informed that he was doing them a favour by letting them live a bit longer and that they had no central nervous system and could not feel pain even if they had sufficient brain power. He might have gotten away with this line of reasoning if he had not candidly added that there were 'plenty of people like that too'.

One of the reasons that Reginald did not get on at school was the fact that he avoided sport wherever possible, and that he even expressed contempt for it. I must say that in this respect he often displayed what almost amounted to courage, persistence and resourcefulness. But in the service of an unpopular cause these otherwise worthy attributes only excited further annoyance among boys and masters alike. As another boy once remarked, "He's a damn good runner, but only when you chase him."

Throughout his school life Reginald was dogged by rumours. The ugliest of these was that he was part-Aboriginal. The headmaster even addressed the assembly on the issue and set everyone's mind at rest, officially at least. There were other stories too, about a relationship with Cook, a supposed social problem and connections with the occult. All totally groundless of course, but nonetheless very hurtful to a young lad.

Though Reginald's parents were among the richest associated with the school he never had any money - not that the boys were supposed to, but they all did - and he never, ever had any supplementary tuck. He had to survive as best he could on the school rations. This was not a cause for a compassionate response from his classmates. He was effectively debarred from the 'black market' as it was known and thus, indeed, from society in general.

Proud to be an Australian

Reginald's life after school, what we know of it, was patchy and colourful, like a poor man's quilt, if you will. His life was basically one of wandering. He was supported by an allowance from his parents that was small enough to prevent him from getting into too much trouble in the wrong places. Bluntly put, he was a remittance man. Or remittance child, perhaps, for he never really grew up. For instance, he never learned to drive a car.

He was a good tractor and plant operator, however, and this seems to have served him well at various times on his travels. Jobs he could get, but he could never settle. Something always came up, trouble of some sort, and he had to move on. There were even a couple of scrapes with the law, including an infamous charge of interfering with livestock which I am pleased to say was unceremoniously thrown out of court on a technicality.

After the tragic accident in which the late Doug Lush was run over by his own bulldozer, Reginald, who had been driving the bulldozer at the time, apparently vanished from the face of the earth. The only other witness, Mrs Fawn Lush could shed no light on his whereabouts or intentions and could only say that he was as distraught as was she herself.

Is Reginald dead?

Who knows? There were many children and youth who went missing in the 1980's. Most were found alive. Some were found dead. A very few were not found at all. Perhaps it is fitting. More may come to light in the future. If it does then let us pray that it is more hopeful than this record of a troubled youth's disturbed imagination.

One final word. It is not inconceivable that one day some ignorant, jumped-up, crypto-intellectual johnny-come-lately, academic bounder will come along and try to claim that the central character in these stories, the so-called 'Uncle Vern', was some kind of modern Sisyphus pushing rocks downhill, a modern Prometheus giving matches to children, some kind of symbol of our times. Well, he certainly is not that. He is nothing but a mountebank, and a living slur on the good name of decent rural folk who are and always have been and always will be the backbone of this great nation of ours.

Sir Pelham Corrie
East Melbourne
October 1993
"Proud To Be Australian"